PARADISE TRIPTYCH

A LOVE STORY IN THREE PARTS

JUDE KNIGHT

TITCHFIELD
PRESS

PART I

PARADISE REGAINED

James yearns to end a long journey in the arms of his loving family. But his father's agents offer the exiled prodigal forgiveness and a place in Society — if he abandons his foreign-born wife and children to return to England.

With her husband away, Mahzad faces revolt, invasion and betrayal in the mountain kingdom they built together. A queen without her king, she will not allow their dream and their family to be destroyed.

JUDE KNIGHT
Paradise Regained
A prequel novella to The Children of the Mountain King
THE KING AND HIS QUEEN

To marriage, and to the one who has been my partner over many years in rekindling the fire from embers.

AUTHOR'S NOTE

This story is set in an entirely imaginary kingdom hidden high in the mountains on the northeast border between Iran and Turkmenistan. Such kingdoms, called *khanates* or *kaganates*, proliferated in the troubled times as one dynasty of Iranian rulers faded and another had not yet come to power.

My story is set in the year that the last Zand ruler died, and the Qajar who would be the first of his dynasty set out to reunify Iran.

At the time, westerners called Iran '*Persia*' after the great empire Alexander the Great conquered more than 2000 years ago, and my hero (who is English) occasionally drops into that term. To those living in Iran, Persia was just one ancient kingdom in what was then called *Eran-shahr* or *Airan-shahr*, which means 'the place of the Aryans'. This evolved to become Iran-shahr and, more recently, just Iran.

James's horse is a Turkmen. His descendants today are Akhal Teke, one of the most beautiful horse breeds in the world, famed for their metallic shine, their endurance and their fierce loyalty.

James's people speak a polyglot language created from various Turkic languages and Persian (or Farsi). I've used their words here and there throughout the story. If you can't tell what I meant, look at the glossary at the back.

کمبل همه چیز برای عشق

The page divider used in this book is a few words in Persian: Gamble everything for love. These are the first few words of a poem from the Persian Sufi philosopher poet Jalal al-Din Muhammad Rumi:

> Gamble everything for love.
>   If you are a true human being.
>   If not, leave this gathering.
>   Half-heartedness doesn't reach into majesty.
>   You set out to find God, but then you keep
> stopping for long periods at mean-spirited roadhouses.
>   Don't wait any longer.
>   Dive in the ocean, leave and let the sea be you.
>   Silent, absent, walking an empty road, all praise.

1

1 *794: Pari-Daiza Vadi in the Kopet Dag Mountains northeast of Iran*
The courtyard had been designed to catch and hold the fickle warmth of the mountain sun. Even in early winter, Mahzad and her ladies chose to settle in the pavilion, out of the direct heat, though the children and their nursemaids played on the paving by the cross-shaped pool at the centre of the garden.

James had ordered it built: a paradise garden on the Persian *chahar bāgh* model, centred on water and divided into four quadrants, each richly planted in vivid colours. It had been her wedding present, and somehow, their tribe had managed to keep it a secret from their queen, though the *qal'a*, the citadel, buzzed with intrigue until James had brought her here, blindfolded.

It had been full summer, and the garden had been glorious but not as beautiful to her eyes as the face of her husband, eyes alight with mischief, with love, and with a promise for later that night when the court was asleep. They had crept down when the *qal'a* fell silent, giggling when the patrolling guards politely averted their eyes. Mahzad was confident their eldest son, Jamie, had been conceived that night.

She had been so in love, had been convinced that James had

forgotten the English woman for whom he was exiled from his home and had fallen in love with her.

Eleven years and eight children later, her love was deeper and stronger than ever, but she no longer believed that James returned the feeling. He was fond of her, yes. He respected her as his wife and queen, *katan* to his *kagan*, but the passion of the soul? No. She reached for it with her own and met only the barrier of blank civility with which he armored himself from the world.

When he was home, he was distant if polite, and he had not been home in more than seven months. His trips away had become longer and longer, his letters home more and more formal. He was about the business of their *kaganate*, which prospered under their rule, but he had never before failed to be home for a birth of one of their children.

Mahzad dropped a kiss on baby Rosemary's dark hair, handed the sleeping baby to the hovering nursemaid, and sent one of her ladies to summon her secretary. She had work to do. She was co-ruler of their people and did not have time to waste mourning the fickleness of men.

The messenger was only halfway down the long side of the garden when Patma came hurrying down the steps from the *zenana*, the women's section of the palace. Even from the other end of the garden, Mahzad could see that her secretary was agitated about something. She had lost the calm she had adopted as chief of Mahzad's scribes, her usual elegant glide abandoned for a walk that bordered on a run, her eyes wide with excitement. She was not surrounded by the bevy of undersecretaries who carried her desk and writing tools, prepared her ink, ran her messages, and made copies of lesser documents.

No. There they were, just stepping out of the long doors onto the *zenana's* terrace. Patma must have hurried some distance to have so outstripped them.

The secretary did not pause when she passed Mahzad's messenger, speaking over her shoulder as she skirted a small child pushing a toy pony and hurried up the steps to the pavilion. She stopped at the top of the steps to kick off her footwear before venturing on to the rugs that lay everywhere and then composed herself enough to offer a polite greeting, bowing as she said, "Peace be upon you, my queen."

"Peace, most excellent of scholars," Mahzad responded, inclining her head as she waited for the younger woman to burst with whatever news she carried.

Patma bowed again. "*Katan, serkerde* Gurban reports possible trouble coming our way from Iran. A caravan, he says, pursued by bandits or possibly soldiers."

Mahzad squelched the fleeting hope that the commander of her forces was in error; that the approaching group was James and his men, returning at last. Gurban would make no such mistake, and besides, James would be coming from north of the mountains, not south. His last letter put him on the shores of the Caspian, the great inland sea that separated the khanates of Turkmenistan from the shifting borders between Russia and Iran in the Caucasian Mountains.

"How large a force?" she asked.

"The *serkerde* says three long strings of camels, and the caravan also has horses and carts. The pursuers are further back, except for those harassing the tail of the caravan. The *serkerde* has sent men to count them, but they must surely have more men than the caravan, do you not think? Or why would it flee?"

"More men, or better armed, or better trained. Is Gurban son of Azat waiting to report to me?" She stood, assuming the answer would be "yes," and kept her face impassive when Patma shook her head.

"He has ridden out with a force to secure the pass, excellency."

"Then we shall follow." Mahzad was already heading for the palace, throwing out orders to send her attending maids scurrying to fetch her riding clothes, her personal guard, her horse.

She was ruler here in her husband's absence. She should have been appraised of the threat by her military commander, should have been the one to decide how to deal with it. Not that she disagreed with his decision. Secure the pass, of course. Keep both sets of intruders out, and settle their differences beyond the valley Mahzad and James protected.

Gurban thought women should engage in the virtues and tasks of the hearth and leave military action and rulership to men. Never mind that Mahzad had fought alongside James since the first bandit attack on their caravan fifteen years ago and been co-ruler with him since they overcame the robber chief who formerly tyrannised this hidden valley. Invited to stay and make it their kingdom, they had renamed it Pari Daiza, the enclosed garden.

Her military commander was loyal to James, but James had been gone a long time. What if…

She shook off her fears. At least he had sent to tell her what was happening.

Which reminded her. "How did you come to carry the *serkerde's* message, Patma?"

"He came to the schoolroom, my lady. To fetch Jamie *beg* and Matthew *beg* to ride with him…" Patma faltered as Mahzad stopped abruptly.

"And?" Mahzad prompted.

"I heard what he told the young princes, my lady, and came to inform you."

Ah, yes. Patma would have been giving the older children their thrice-weekly lessons in calligraphy. Mahzad lengthened her stride so her court had to hurry to catch up. If Patma had not been giving that lesson, Gurban would have carried off Mahzad's two eldest sons with Mahzad none the wiser.

Gurban son of Azat had gone too far.

کمبل همه چیز برای عشق

A fishing port on the west coast of the Caspian Sea

"I should have been home months ago," James complained. He had been rereading the letter that kept him tethered in this Caspian Sea port, as if it would miraculously change and disclose the reason he was being asked to wait. Hints about his father and news to his advantage? The Duke of Winshire never did anything to anyone's advantage but his own.

"We could not travel in this weather, and when the storm is over, your father's men will be able to cross the sea," his body guard Yousef pointed out.

James tossed the letter into the top of the open pack that held his clothes. The one next to it, with the odd bumpy protrusions, was packed tightly with presents for Mahzad and the children, some to celebrate his homecoming and some for Christmas which was mere weeks away.

Toys. Books. Swords. He and Mahzad had agreed the two older boys were ready for real weapons, half-sized to suit their height. Matthew, in particular, had an instinct for sword craft, both the Eastern and the Western style.

The small swords commissioned from a Spanish master sword maker might be a little large, depending on how quickly the boys had grown in the months he'd been away. The largest of the three blades was intended not for his sons but for his wife, a beautiful weapon, graceful, elegant, and deadly. Mahzad would love it.

"The *begum's* last letter said she was well," Yousef added, which set James pacing again, for in Mahzad's last letter, she had reminded him her time was almost on her. As if she thought he didn't know. As if he wasn't counting the days.

The date on her letter was weeks ago, and still, he lingered here more than two hundred miles from home. He had never before missed the birth of one of their children.

"The baby will be born by now."

Someone would write, surely, if things had gone wrong? His tortured visions of his Mahzad dying in childbed and his children killed or sold to slavers were nonsense.

Yousef, who had begun as his jailor nearly two decades ago and become his best friend, easily followed his thoughts. "The son of Azat is a reliable man, and the people are loyal."

Peter was busy polishing a high shine into the Western style boots James had purchased in Italy. As always, he took a gloomier view. "Childbirth is a chancy business," he intoned.

James usually ignored his valet's determination to see the clouds behind every silver lining, but today's remark matched his own imaginings too closely for comfort.

Yousef snorted. "Mahzad *begum* has birthed seven children without difficulty, and they know where we are. If she needs our lord, a fast rider would reach us in two days. Three at most."

Which means, James thought, *that Mahzad doesn't need me, which I already knew.*

Oh, they still worked together well, and she always treated him with courtesy, even affection. But she was so busy with the children, with the business of the kingdom. Even in their bed, she seemed to be thinking about something else.

That had been at least part of the motivation for this long trip. Only a small part. Someone had to check a possible shipping venture as a sound way to invest the wages he and his people had earned guarding caravans through the mountain passes. He was the best person for the job, since he spoke the languages of the places in the Mediterranean where they'd need to go to secure docking-rights and had friends in most of the them. He was English, which wasn't ideal in Italy and France, but certainly more to his motley tribe's advantage than sending a Persian or Turkmen to deal with people in those countries. The land route to avoid the Ottoman Empire meant learning Russian, but he'd always picked up languages quickly.

"I am going to check on the horses," he announced. Anything to take his mind of the endless waiting.

Yousef fell into step behind him as he crossed the outer room where most of their party lounged at their ease, dicing or drinking tea. One or two made to rise to their feet, but Yousef waved them down.

In this benighted hole of a fishing village, the only inn took no more than fifty guests and their animals and was currently less than half full. It was built on the *caravanserai* model, a series of interlinked courtyards, each lined with rooms and niches.

James led the way down the stairs, along halls, and through repeated arches until they came out into the large outer courtyard, surrounded by a long colonnade of arches that led to stabling and other housing for riding and pack animals. Melegush was tethered where he could see the courtyard, and he whickered imperatively as the two men approached.

"My golden one," James greeted him.

He had raised the horse from a foal, and there was a deep affection between them not marred by the months Melegush had spent in Astrakhan waiting for James to return from his mission. And providing stud services in partial payment of his board, which Melegush had undoubtedly taken as no more than his due.

Yousef saluted his own horse, and the two men settled to grooming their animals.

"If these agents of my father are not here by the end of the week, they can wait till next Spring," James said. "I'm not missing Christmas with my family for the old man's convenience."

"News to your advantage," Yousef mused. "What could it be, I wonder?"

From the next bay in the colonnade came the jingle of harness and the hum of voices speaking in Turkmen. Melegush and the other horses were about to have neighbours.

James switched to English to answer Yousef's question. "I neither know nor care. It will be to the duke's advantage, not mine."

"An Englishman? Here?"

The speaker stood in the archway, far more incongruous in this setting than the dark-haired James in his robes. An Englishwoman, and not just any Englishwoman but, by the few words she had spoken, one of his own class. Taller than average, with the fair hair so prized here in the middle-East, probably only her age had kept her from being snapped up as a concubine for some local despot. He'd put her in her late thirties or early forties, about the same age as himself, though time had been relatively kind to them both. Here, on the western coast of the Caspian Sea, in a small Turkmen fishing village, she wore a Western carriage dress, riding boots, and a pert bowl-shaped hat with a nonsense of a veil.

James recalled his manners and bowed, a slight inclination,

playing her words back to her with an ironic quirk of his brows. "An Englishwoman? Here?"

That earned him a laugh, and he revised his estimate of her safety as the humour transformed her face, stripping away the years. He hoped she had plenty of guards and the money to keep them loyal.

In the next moment, she narrowed her brows, peering intently at him. "James? Lord James Winderfield? But it cannot be!"

Someone who'd known him? And well enough to call him by his first name? There was something familiar about her, but he couldn't call it to mind.

"Because I am rumoured to be dead?" he asked.

"Yes." The lady nodded. "Eleanor was heartbroken."

Even after all these years, his own heart caught at the thought of Eleanor. She suffered? But then, she had married the Duke of Haverford, and undoubtedly, his wealth and position had been a comfort. *No. That was unfair.* With James gone and her father and his two ducal friends pushing for the alliance, what choice did she have?

James spread his hands. "I am not dead."

"Evidently. Then why…" She caught back whatever she had been about to say. "You don't remember me, do you? Cecily Warren, I was back then. Cecily McInnes, now."

Ah. He did remember. In those days, his attention had been all for Eleanor Creydon, younger daughter of the Earl of Farnmouth, youngest debutante and reigning beauty of the Season. Perforce, he had met the circle of other girls she had gathered around her, generously sharing her success. In the mature woman before him, he saw traces of the gawky girl he remembered, an awkward leggy filly not yet grown into the unconscious grace and beauty Eleanor wore as her birthright.

He remembered Alec McInnes, too, another of Eleanor's suitors. Without rank, wealth, or looks to recommend him, poor Alec had never been in serious contention. As it turned out, nor had any of them, Falmouth having made his diabolical compact with Haverford before Eleanor ever stepped into a ballroom.

"Is Alec with you?" he asked, and was sorry when a wash of pain swept over her face before being absorbed by her studied calm.

"Alec has been gone for almost two decades, Lord James." She lowered her chin and looked up at him through her lashes. "I am a widow."

Flirting had not been one of Cecily Warren's talents as a young woman, but she had clearly had some practice in the last twenty years. Time to remind the lady that they were not alone.

"Mrs. McInnes, allow me to present my friend, Yousef ibn Ahmed. Yousef, Mrs. McInnes is an old friend from my youth."

Cecily could not quite hide the flash of surprised shock, as if he had introduced her to his horse, but she recovered smoothly, dropping a shallow curtsey. "I am pleased to meet you, Mr. Ahmed. Or is it Mr. Yousef?"

Yousef's eyes gleamed, and he bent closer, as if to impart a secret. "Let us solve the conundrum, Mrs. McInnes, by being friends. Yousef will do."

She flushed and dimpled at Yousef's clear interest. "Then you must call me Cecily, Yousef, as must you, James, and we shall be friends together."

Let them flirt with one another and leave him out of it, James thought, but he gave a half smile in agreement and allowed himself to be persuaded to join Yousef in escorting the lady to her rooms and checking the disposition of her guard.

"How fortunate for me that you were here," she said.

Which raised the question of the reason behind her presence, which seemed highly unlikely. But such a chatty woman would undoubtedly tell all if he gave her half a chance. James had only to wait.

کمبل همه چیز برای عشق

Cecily allowed herself an inward smile of congratulation as she prattled about the discomforts of her trip around the southern shores of the Caspian Sea. Step one of her mission was accomplished. Lord James Winderfield was precisely where she had been told, and she had made contact. Before she had been ten minutes in the *caravanserai*, in fact!

He was even more handsome than he'd been twenty years ago. Seducing him would not be a chore, though it was a pity about his friend, who was even more to her taste. Perhaps they could be persuaded to share? But that would not suit the plan, would it? She needed to remember what was at stake and not allow herself to be distracted.

2

Pari-Daiza Vadi

Gurban and her two sons were atop the wall James had ordered built in the narrow winding pass that was the main entry to their valley. Mahzad ignored the pull in unused muscles as she climbed the stair, grateful for her mare's easy gait and the relatively short distance between the palace and the pass. She had not been on a horse since her seventh month of pregnancy, but she would be sure to make time for riding after today.

She forced her steps into a graceful glide, pleased to see the welcome on the faces of her two boys and most of the other men. She was still *katan*, the queen, mother, and heroine of the people, though most of those on this wall were too young to remember how she and James defeated their oppressor and set them free.

Gurban's eyebrows nearly met as he frowned, even as he shifted from one foot to another and shot a glance sideways at his officers. Annoyed and nervous, was he? Mahzad could work with that.

She smiled. "Peace be upon you, *serkerde*, and thank you for your devotion to the people." At the acknowledgement of his rank and purpose, some of the tension went from his shoulders. "I received your message and have come straight away. Do we know yet who these strangers are?"

There. Now embarrass me and yourself in front of my sons and the men or take my lead.

He was no fool, the *serkerde*. "Peace be upon you, Lady. No, though both groups are dressed and armed in the Persian style."

"Look, Mama," said young Jamie. "The camels keep coming, though they must see us here on the wall. What should we do?"

"Keep them all out, of course," Matthew answered, scornfully. "Should we not, Mama?"

Another palm leaf for Gurban. "*Serkerde*? Has this young warrior the right of it?"

As she waited for his answer, she unslung her bow. She was accomplished enough with a blade, thanks to many hours of tutoring by the children's father, but unmatched with the bow. If the intruders thought to enter the valley, she would help to change their minds.

Gurban read her intent, and a reluctant smile pulled at the corner of his lips. "Matthew *beg* is correct," he pronounced, more to his soldiers than to her sons, "as is our *katan*. She has her bow at the ready."

"Ho the gate!" The shout, in Persian, confirmed the origin of the caravan. The first camel had emerged from the twisting path, coming out onto the flat patch before the gate twenty yards away, its rider cupping his hand as he bellowed.

Gurban confirmed that Mahzad had won at least this challenge to her authority by looking to her for permission to respond. She nodded, and he moved forward, gesturing as he went so that several of the guard moved to put themselves and their shields between the intruders' possible arrows and Mahzad and her sons. *Well thought, Gurban.*

"What seek you in the valley of the mountain king?" Gurban shouted.

He spoke Persian clearly, if with a Turkmen accent. Indeed, their people were polyglot by necessity, reflecting their many origins: Turkmen, Persian, Chinese, Mughal, Arab, Caucasian, and even

African, as well as their English leader. The original valley people were already of mixed ancestry. The guard who had absconded with her and James from the service of her father added an even wider mix, since most had been slaves captured in pirate or military adventures from the far edges of the Muslim world. Many others—Silk Road travellers and local tribespeople—had chosen to join them as they made a success of guarding the caravans that crossed or skirted the mountains.

"Refuge and sanctuary," the herald called back.

Gurban signaled for his archers to put arrow to bow and aim. "Return the way you came."

"We are pursued," the herald shouted, looking back along the mountain trail.

Those chasing them were not yet in view, but the herald's own party had now all reached the empty space before the gate, carefully altered by James's engineers to be within bow shot of walls and without cover.

The herald seemed to realise this, shrinking a little as if to make himself a smaller target then stretching out again. "We come in peace."

"You have no business here," Gurban said sternly. "Return the way you came. Take your enemies with you."

One of the camels was kneeling, and someone was being helped to the ground, a woman so wrapped in a chador that even her gender was a deduction. The herald turned his camel, which strode toward her as she hurried through the waiting crowd. From the wall, they couldn't hear his words, but his tone was enough to suggest argument. One that he lost, for the woman pressed forward.

Gurban raised his arm, ready to give the signal to fire.

"Wait," Mahzad said, whether out of curiosity or premonition, she could not have said.

Gurban frowned but obeyed.

The woman stopped just a few feet from the foremost of the camels, her servants hovering behind her.

"Mahzad," she shouted, in English. "Mahzad, is that you? It is Grandmother. I have come to visit."

کمبل همه چیز برای عشق

Caspian Sea coast

"We are going home," Yousef explained to Cecily, who had joined them for dinner at their fire, bringing her chief guard with her. James was happy to let him carry the burden of the conversation, while James brooded about the distance that still separated him from his family.

Yousef was also yearning for the valley. "We left in the spring, and it is now winter. It will be good to be at our own hearths again."

"Home," she said, with a sigh. She looked down at the signet ring she wore on the middle finger of her left hand, a man's ring surely, and an old one too, gold and crowned in a star. "A star to lead you home." Looking up, she met James's eyes. "The promise of the ring. It is from Viking times, or so they say, and is meant to be good luck for travellers." More quietly, she added, "I, too, have been away from home for a long time."

"What adventures bring you here, Cecily?" James asked. He had been burning with curiosity all afternoon. Had McInnes left her with enough wealth to travel? He would not have thought so, though she may have had other wealthy relatives to endow her in twenty years.

She chuckled, the wistful expression on her face disappearing as if it had never existed. "Too long a tale for such an evening, Lord James. We would be here all night, you and Yousef asleep from boredom, long before I was done."

As she had all evening, she ignored Peter and her own guard, a Turk from Istanbul called Kamal. The Turkmen habit of regarding all men as equal, and of treating servants as family, was much more to James's taste, but she could not help her upbringing. He would try not to hold it against her.

"Suffice it to say," she continued, "that I left home to broaden my horizons, and I am now ready to return to England." She turned to Yousef, leaning slightly toward him, and James was amused to realise she was trying to make him jealous. "I love the

East, Yousef, but I miss my own land. I miss the green hills and the trees and flowers of home. I even miss the rain."

"Have you been to Persia, Cecily?" Yousef asked. "You would love the gardens of Persia."

"Persia, Lebanon, Turkey, Egypt." Cecily sighed. "They all have their beauties. None of them are home."

Yousef quoted the thirteenth century Sufi poet, Jalāl al-Dīn Rūmī.

"I burst my breast, striving to give vent to sighs, and to express the pangs of my yearning for my home. He who abides far away from his home is ever longing for the day he shall return."

Cecily laughed, a light studied tinkle of a sound. "You must translate for me. I fear my grasp of Persian is insufficient."

But sufficient enough to know that, of all possible languages, Yousef the Egyptian had spoken Persian.

Yousef obliged with the translation, and Cecily's eyes lit in a smile.

"Just so," she agreed.

James had clearly spent too long with connivers and tricksters, when he suspected a chance met Englishwoman—an old friend, furthermore—of lying about how well she spoke Persian. The Persian poets were the best in the world, or so said the Persians. And she would know that, if she'd travelled as broadly as she said. He shook off his doubts, although with a mental note to assume he and his party could not discuss secrets in front of Cecily in any language.

"How far to your home?" Cecily addressed the question to Yousef.

He answered easily but in general terms. A vague wave to the South West. The number of days' easy ride. Yousef waxed lyrical about crossing the desert in the spring, and James grumbled that they should have been home long since. The Turkmenistan desert in early winter could be a bleak place. They would need to carry all the feed for their animals and travel fast in the hopes of avoiding being caught by a storm.

"Ah." Cecily nodded, twisting the Viking ring to and fro on her finger. "You have been away longer than you intended. I likewise, but your home is merely a few days ride, gentlemen. I have much further to go. Still, I daresay to be away so long you have travelled far? To Egypt, perhaps?"

"To Egypt, the Hellenes, Lebanon. Even Spain and Algeria," Yousef boasted, preening a little under the Englishwoman's flirtatious gaze.

There was no reason for James to find that annoying. She was a widow and Yousef a single man, both of them adults. If they found one another attractive, it was none of James's business. Any concern he might feel was simply as a friend to them both.

"A long trip," she observed. "No wonder you have been away so long."

That prompted Yousef to tell some of their adventures: being blown off course, fighting corsairs, negotiating their freedom with the Turks and later the Italians. Their accommodations in Istanbul were more comfortable and the Ottoman officials more courteous, but Yousef still had fond memories of the Italian prison guard's daughter.

Cecily listened with every evidence of enjoyment, occasionally turning with sparkling eyes to James to ask him a question or make a comment. When they finally parted for their beds, James was surprised to discover how quickly the evening had passed.

3

P*ari-Daiza Vadi*

Mamani, Mahzad's grandmother, made herself at home in Mahzad's garden, her own ladies and maids hovering around her. She had grown old and frail in the fifteen years since they last met, but was still every inch Mahroch *begum*, formerly Lady Emma Finstanley, the imperious English lady who had ruled her son's *zenana* with a firm but compassionate hand.

"Ask for anything you wish, *Mamani*," Mahzad told her.

"It is your home, dearest," she insisted. "I do not want to inconvenience you in the slightest. But if I could just have my couch moved a little out of the breeze…"

Mahzad distracted her by bringing the children to be introduced, admired, and fussed over.

Mahzad's father Garshasp was less easily managed. He had made himself known, stepping out from among the ranks of the camel drivers once the gates were firmly shut between his caravan and the pursuing soldiers. They were Qajar troops, loyal to Mohammad Khan, whom James had long picked as the likely winner of the struggle for Iran.

Garshasp had bathed, shaved, and dressed once more in the

princely robes of a *khan*, *khan*, furthermore, of a province left almost independent by the disintegration of Zand Iran. He graciously forgave his daughter for escaping his control twenty years ago. He then began giving orders for the defence of the valley from the soldiers he'd brought down upon them.

"At least," Mahzad whispered to baby Rosemary as she fed her, "Gurban is firmly my supporter again. Even a woman is better than an arrogant Persian interloper."

She could hear the arrogant Persian interloper at the doors, the guards firmly telling him that he could not enter the women's quarters of the palace.

"Is this not my daughter's house?" he demanded. "I am master here."

"Our *kagan* is master here, and our *katan* is his deputy in his absence," one of the guardsmen replied. Luka. He had been a slave with James and would walk through hell for the man who returned to him his freedom and his dignity. The *Khan* would not be entering today.

"Go to the doors," Mahzad told one of the older maids, "and ask my father to wait for me in the audience rooms. Arrange for food and drink to be served. Tell him I am feeding his granddaughter but will come as soon as I can."

She sent more messages, for this was unlikely to be a fond reunion between father and daughter. Her grandmother had once before chosen to support Mahzad rather than Garshasp *Khan*. Perhaps she would again. The others were her own people, hers and James's. Patma as her secretary. For secular wisdom, the village headman and the wise woman, as well as Gurban *serkerde*. For spiritual guidance, the priest of the small Chaldean Christian Church and the *mojtahed* who ruled in their little mosque. The two men were fierce chess opponents, warm friends, and devoted allies in the welfare of the village.

She arrived to find her father and Gurban glaring at one another, while Patma cowered behind Gurban.

Garshasp spun toward her, his voice booming in the tone that used to frighten her into obedience when she was a child.

"Daughter, this man of yours has offered me insult. I want him whipped."

Gurban made to protest but shut his mouth at Mahzad's gesture. She sank gracefully onto the pillows scattered around the seating area of the room and beckoned Patma to her. The girl scurried to her side, her eyes wide with fright.

"Are you hurt, my dear?" Mahzad asked.

Garshasp raised his voice again, "Daughter, this man—"

Mahzad made the shushing gesture again, not turning to look at her father. "Patma?"

"No, *begum*. The *serkerde* came before his excellency…"

Mahzad gave the trembling girl a hug, just as a bustle at the doors announced the arrival of the people from the village. Gurban raised his brows, and Mahzad nodded, sending him to ask them to wait a moment.

With only Patma as witness, who deserved to hear, Mahzad said, "Great Khan," his formal title, "I will require none of the women under my protection to warm your bed. Not the lady Patma, not the least of my maidservants. As it is, you have frightened and attempted to molest the daughter of one of the most powerful men in these parts and insulted me and my husband, since we promised her parents we would care for her as if she were our own daughter. You owe a debt to the *serkerde*, who prevented you from committing an even worse offence."

Garshasp opened his mouth. By the gleam in his eye and the lift of his chin, he was ready to argue, but Gurban was ushering in the valley leaders, spiritual and temporal, and he subsided. The door opened again, and Grandmother glided in, hurrying forward when she saw the others were before her.

Mahzad hissed, "Let us leave this private family matter until later." She pitched her voice to be heard throughout the room and began the introductions.

کمبل همه چیز برای عشق

Caspian Sea Coast

"I saw a magpie," Peter announced mournfully. "Just one, my lord."

"Indeed."

James was barely listening. A break in the weather had tempted him out for a ride, and he had returned to news that another Englishman had arrived at the *caravanserai*. The man had asked after Jakob beg Pari-daiza, not Lord James Winderfield, so it might not be his father's agent. James had used his Eastern name and title only in Turkey when he visited this year, not while in the European countries, nor had he written it on the letter of condolence he'd sent his father after he had heard his brother Edward had died.

On the off chance the man was not from the Duke of Winshire, James washed and dressed in the mix of Turkmen and Persian clothing most of his people preferred.

"One for sorrow," Peter reminded him, reaching out to fasten the tightly fitted neck-high silk overcoat.

James brushed away his valet's hands. "But whose sorrow, Peter? My father's? He has lost a son, after all."

Peter shook his head. "Three people passed me on the stair when I came back from fetching water, my lord. Three! We cannot expect this meeting to turn out well."

James, who was nervous about the coming encounter, was not as sympathetic as usual. "You had better stay here, then, Peter, since the ill luck seems to be targeting you."

He left his valet touching wood and muttering about a black cat in the stables, which would bring good luck if he could only persuade it to allow him to stroke it.

A servant escorted James to the meeting, Yousef at his shoulder. Two men waited in an inner room on the highest level of the *caravanserai*. A fire kept the place almost too warm and rugs brightened the floor. The flickering light from lamps and the fire didn't disguise the shabbiness of the furniture. Western chairs! Had the *caravanserai* dug them up from somewhere? Or did this pair carry them with them?

The younger man, fair haired and clean shaven, was getting to his feet, and the other, burlier and bearded, reluctantly followed.

"Lord James Winderfield?" The fair man offered a welcoming smile and a handshake. The accent was English and carefully educated.

James took the offered hand, a firm and business-like grasp and still the man smiled, baring his teeth.

"I am. And you, sir?"

"Gerald Redding, my lord, but most people call me Gerry. Very much at your service. And at your father's, of course."

That settled that question. James prepared himself to resist the long-distance machinations of the Duke of Winshire.

Redding was continuing with the introductions. "This is my colleague, Nikolai Michaelov."

The Russian offered his hand, and James found himself in a subtle wrestling match, smiling into the dark eyes as he returned the grip with interest.

James completed the introductions. "My friend, Yousef ibn Ahmed."

Redding blinked but showed no more surprise, greeting Yousef as enthusiastically as he had James. Michaelov repeated his strength test with similar results.

"I will send for another chair," Redding announced.

James politely refused. "I have spent two decades in the East, Mr. Redding, and am accustomed to sitting on cushions."

Redding declared himself delighted, following James's and Yousef's example in dropping to the floor, but Michaelov, scowling, declared he would take a chair if no one else did.

"Coffee, my lord?" Redding asked, waving to a table where a spirit stove and pot stood waiting.

James and Yousef accepted and followed Redding's lead in a general conversation about the weather and the scenery and the discomfort of a trip in a fishing boat across the Caspian Sea.

What was Father's link with Russia? James had chosen the route across the Caspian Sea and through Russia and Ukraine to avoid the Ottoman Empire and stay in Christian lands. Was Mikhailov's presence unconnected? *Time would tell, but let them be the first to speak of the business that brought them here.*

Somewhere, Redding had learned to make good coffee in the Eastern style, even providing sugar cubes to put between one's teeth through which to suck the rich bitter liquid from the tiny cups he produced from a case.

Michaelov shifted restlessly as he accepted his cup and said in Russian, "Give him the letter, and let's get this over with, Zjerry."

Nothing in James's face or Yousef's would have given the pair a clue that James spoke a little Russian and understood a lot more.

"Can we speak in English, please?" he asked to secure the advantage. "Or I also speak Farsi and Turkmen."

"Also Italian, French, and Spanish, or so I am told," Redding gushed. "So many languages! I suppose they have been useful in your travels? They tell me you have been securing harbour rights for ships. Do you have a large fleet?"

Was this interest from the duke? Or did his agents have other irons in the fire? Still, what Redding had said so far was no secret.

"Moderate," James replied. "An investment with a group of friends."

Yousef, one of the friends, shifted to clear the way to the dagger he wore under his robes. Yousef, too, felt the hostility radiating off the Russian.

Enough. "You have a message for me, I believe, Mr. Redding."

"Yes, of course." Redding dug into the bag from which he had already taken the jar with the coffee and the case with the cups to produce a folded document plain but for the name J. Winderfield and heavy encrustations of wax marked with the Winshire seal.

"The duke's letter, my lord. Also," he reached again into the bag, "one from your sister, Lady Georgiana."

James took the letters, tucking them inside his robe, and then stood. "Thank you, gentlemen. I appreciate your coming so far to deliver these. I hope my father paid you well."

"Oh, but…" Redding caught back whatever else he was about to say, and Michaelov just scowled.

"I would lay you any kinds of odds," James murmured to Yousef as they threaded the halls back to their own rooms, "that they have been paid to take me back to England." He laughed. "Not without an army. Not here so close to our own lands."

As expected, the duke's letter was a demand for James to return to England immediately. "You are now third in line. Your brother's wife has given him only three children, two of them useless girls, and nothing for years. The boy is sickly, so there is every chance you will step into my shoes after Sutton."

James shuddered at the thought. His eldest brother, the Earl of Sutton, had been the Duke of Winshire's pet, his lap dog and his whipping boy for as long as James could remember, under constant surveillance, never allowed an independent thought or action.

He turned to his sister's letter. It was a passionate plea for him to return to England, the emotional turns of phrase highly unlike the contained and dignified Lady Georgiana he remembered. Either she had changed or… yes, there it was. The little English rose carefully inscribed as a decoration to the salutation. What follows meant the opposite of what it said.

James searched the letter. All of the sentences had symbols instead of full stops, most of them roses but here and there a tiny heart, which meant what follows is true.

He read the letter again. She was thrilled to know he lived. If he came home, their father would have him married and breeding almost before he hit the shore. She would love it if he could find a way to write. She then gave him one, clever girl.

"Rose symbol. Of course, when you come home, you will not need to write. Heart symbol. Do you remember Henry Redepenning? He is a general with the Horse Guard and a dear friend."

The letter was signed "Lady Georgiana Winderfield." So, Georgie had successfully resisted their father's attempts to marry her to his advantage. Good for her.

کمبل همه چیز برای عشق

James had met with Gerry and Nikolai. Cecily had watched from her own rooms as Gerry let him and his handsome friend in and then farewelled them. She could read nothing from James's expression, but Gerry was clearly upset, though he should not be surprised. She had warned them that James never did what was expected. He hadn't as a young man, and why would twenty years of independence have changed that?

She needed him to go back to England and to take her with him. Nikolai's master, the Russian Ambassador to the Ottoman Court, had purchased her from her Turkish protector and promised her freedom if she helped secure the English lordling. She had thought of running as soon as she was away from Nikolai's constant surveillance, but where would she go? Freedom was a good start but wouldn't last without a ticket home and money to live on once she arrived.

She was so tired of depending on the whims of a man, though she would make an exception for James Winderfield. She'd always liked him, but he'd only had eyes for Eleanor Creydon. Perhaps he would keep her as a mistress. Perhaps, if she played her cards right, she could even be his wife. Wouldn't that be one in the eye for all those who had despised her for her inability to win status within a *seraglio* by producing a son for any of her various masters?

4

Pari-Daiza Vadi

"I am so proud of you, Mahzad," *Mamani* said. "Eight children and four of them sons! The mother of a son has power, my love. You shall rule through one of them when he succeeds his father."

Mahzad did not argue that such a result depended on her living longer than James, and she would not wish to live were he not in the world. *Mamani* was proud of her son, but all her love was for the granddaughter given to her to raise after the death of the Khan's Chinese concubine.

Mamani ignored her silence. "A daughter is a token for her father to use. A wife can have some small influence until some other female catches her husband's interest. But the mother of a son!" *Mamani* clapped her hands. "She has power, Mahzad. The child who fed at her breast, whose first words she heard, who praised his accomplishments and mourned with him at his losses. He will listen to his mother."

It was one of *Mamani's* favourite sayings, last heard when Mahzad had threatened open rebellion at the news her father intended to use her to buy the favour of the most powerful contender for the throne of Iran in the civil war that followed the death of Karim Khan. Ali-Morād Khan Zand planned a diplomatic mission to the East, all the way to China, seeking allies by giving gifts, and he expected his supporters to provide treasures, including concubines and wives, for the expedition.

کمبل همه چیز برای عشق

1779: North Khorisan Province, Iran

"You will be destined for the Emperor's own women's quarters, Mahzad," *Mamani* said. "As a wife, no less. Just imagine! Your son could be Emperor."

Only, Mahzad wanted to say, if they could successfully avoid trouble in the broken lands that had once been the Uzbek empire. Only if she had sons. Only if one of those sons survived the machinations of the *zenana* and then of the *divan*, the government bureaucracy, to become ruler. She had no intention of putting all her faith in a child as yet not even conceived, but she could clearly expect no support from her grandmother, so she said nothing.

She was not the only high-ranking trophy bride in the caravan. They would negotiate their way East, giving gifts to the rulers of kingdoms and cities along the way, and most of the other girls felt as she did.

"But what can we do?" asked Fatimah, daughter of a satrap and his Uzbekistan concubine and therefore probably the first to be traded for the safety of the caravan. "That Englishman of your grandmother's has us closely watched."

Fatimah was another favoured daughter, allowed freedoms and training beyond the feminine arts, petted and praised by her father, and then sent to be used with as little compunction as if she were a pawn of ivory or jet, rather than flesh and blood.

"How much do you wish to escape?" Mahzad asked.

In the end, nine of them made the attempt, including Mahzad's maid. The other three promised to cover for them and helped them gather the men's clothes they would wear to avoid the risks of women travelling without a male escort.

Their chance came after a bandit attack in the mountains. The would-be robbers were killed or driven off, and the triumphant guard relaxed around their fires, celebrating their success, while Mahzad and her friends followed the English *serveries'* instructions to stay in their tent. "Drunk men may forget themselves, princess," he told her. "And I would not wish to have to cut off a man's hand because one of you failed to hide when I told you to."

After midnight, as the noise around the men's fires died down, the runaway brides kissed their friends goodbye. They had long since sent their maids off to bed, and now, they helped one another into their new clothes, shushing one another's giggles as they struck male poses.

They were nine slim lads, gliding through the shadows to the horse pickets, where the guards, praise be to all the saints, nodded over a jug of wine.

Each woman saddled and bridled her own horse, and Mahzad breathed another prayer of thanks. Some of them had never waited on themselves in their whole pampered lives. The travel and the English *serkerde's* insistence that they each learn to do some of the daily tasks, such as looking after their own horses, had hardened them and readied them for this adventure.

Mahzad was about to give the order to mount when one of the guards lifted his head and spoke.

"Going somewhere, princess?"

Startled, she could do nothing but stare into the face of the Englishman who commanded the caravan. Jakob. James, as his own people said it. In that frozen moment, the other three guards moved, standing and raising their weapons.

The other brides looked to Mahzad. *For orders or for inspiration?* She raised her chin. She was descended from royal houses in China, Persia, Turkmenistan, and England, and would not give up.

"You are four, and we are nine," she pointed out. "We are leaving, James *Beg*."

"I am impressed," he replied, and his eyes gleamed. "I would not have thought of men's clothes."

"We are leaving," she repeated, clutching at her mare's reins until the horse sidled.

"Princess, I made a promise to your grandmother that I would defend you against all dangers. How can I do that if I let you leave?"

"You are four, and we are nine," she repeated, but even she was unconvinced. Nine pampered ladies who had never used their weapons in earnest against four hardened warriors?

"Forgive me. I have not made myself clear. If I let you leave without me, I should have said. But I have no more desire than you ladies," he bowed to include them all, "to continue with this mission now it has brought us within reach of our freedom. Will you consent to take us as partners in your escape?"

كمبل همه چيز براى عشق

1794, Caspian Sea coast

James regarded the Russian and the Englishman across the delicately hand-knotted silk and woolen rug. He may have made a tactical error in wearing European clothes. He'd thought to emphasise to Redding and Michaelov that he was English and a duke's son and to be treated with respect. Instead, they appeared to have taken the message that he was ready to abandon the life he had built here in the Middle East and crawl back to accept whatever crumbs fell from his father's table.

Their contempt and condescension grew as the interview, if you could call it that when he sat silent and impassive, continued.

At his shoulder, Yousef bristled with anger on his behalf, but he would do nothing without James's signal.

"You can be sure of the prodigal's welcome," Redding said, folding his hands across an incipient paunch with a smug smile. "Your father is prepared to forgive all and to welcome you with the fatted calf."

Forgive him? For what? For being exiled? For continuing to live after he was imprisoned by the Persians and his father refused to pay the ransom? For certain, Garshasp Khan would have had him beheaded or at least castrated if the man's mother had not been English and ready to intervene on a fellow countryman's behalf by pointing out that James had weapons skills that made him valuable to the Khan's guard.

James inclined his head at Redding's nonsensical comment, a noncommittal sign but one Michaelov took as agreement.

"And you may yet be duke, Lord James. Lord Sutton has only the one son, and he is a sickly boy. With Lord Edward's death, you are third in line."

Time to end this.

"I have four sons," James told them, "and three daughters." And another child by now, whose birth he had missed, thanks to the troubles they had encountered and a further delay to meet these idiots. "I take it that my father is willing to accept Lady James and our children with the same enthusiasm?"

Not likely and the expressions on the faces of his father's men confirmed it.

"Lady James?" Redding said cautiously. "Your native wife, is it?"

His Mahzad, royal in all her bloodlines, every inch a princess and the holder of his heart, though that organ did not appear to be as essential to her as the children and the kingdom they shared. If he were to abandon good sense and his duty to their people and traipse back to England to live on his father's erratic goodwill, he had very little hope she would come with him.

After that, the meeting broke up fairly quickly. Redding did a good job of hiding his shock that James would put his "native wife" ahead of the supposed advantages of being possible heir to a duke, but Michaelov showed open disdain, and James left before he lost his temper.

"We'll leave as soon as we can pack, Yousef," James said as they arrived back in their room.

"Carefully, my lord," Peter warned. "They have a force of armed men just outside the village."

James raised his brows. "Good to know. How big a force, and how did you find out?"

"I went to find the black cat I spoke of, my lord. Sure enough, it brought us good luck, though I did not think so when it walked away from me, staying just out of reach until we left the *caravanserai* and crossed the whole of the village. Then, it dived behind a wall, and when I went after them, I heard them say your name, Winderfield, so I hid and listened."

"Just as well for us, Peter," Yousef agreed. "What did you hear?"

Peter explained that the men were itching for action, since they'd been lying in wait for several days. "But Michaelov said you were going to come of your own accord, so they wouldn't be needed, and they were complaining about having to camp out in the fields in the cold."

James asked a few more questions about the disposition of the men and the number. "We leave tonight, as quietly as possible, after the *caravanserai* is asleep," he decided. "Yousef, let the men know. Once we are out in the desert, no one will catch our horses."

He left Peter to pack up the room and Yousef to organise the men while he wrote a note for Redding to take to the duke a few conciliatory words. If he had to go back to England one day to be duke, as well to leave the door open.

کمبل همه چیز برای عشق

"You are leaving, James?" Cecily McInnes stepped in front of them as they led their horses through the quiet *caravanserai* toward the main gate.

"I am going home," James affirmed.

"Your meeting has been successful, then, but can we not travel together? I, too, am returning to England."

"I am not going to England." James pointed to the southwest, in the general direction of his mountains. "My home is with my wife and my children."

Cecily's face fell, and then she brightened again. "Take me with you. I have… I would be willing, James. I have always liked you."

What brought that on? She had been determined on returning to England mere seconds ago. Whatever her reasons, her proposition was impossible, and he said so.

"I am honoured by your interest but must refuse your offer. I am a married man, Cecily."

She dismissed the objection with a wave of the hand. "To an eastern woman. They understand these things. Are you telling me you do not keep a harem? That does not sound like the rake who set England chattering from his school days."

"I have not been that boy for more than a score of years," James pointed out. Not, in fact, since he had met this woman's close friend, Eleanor. "I made vows before the altar and have kept them these fifteen years."

And would keep them until he died, however Mahzad felt about him, because what was a man worth if he did not keep his word?

"No, Cecily, I cannot take you with me."

She took a deep breath. "You are happy, then, James? I wish you to be happy."

He took a moment to find an answer that honoured his wife and was not untrue. "I am content. I wish happiness to you, too, Cecily. It has been good to meet you again."

Yousef and Peter had waited quietly, staying out of their parting conversation, but now Yousef passed James, followed by Peter, each leading a pair of riding horses and a pack horse. James gave Cecily a final nod of farewell and then braced himself just in time to catch her as she threw herself into his arms and pressed an urgent kiss to his mouth.

He held himself rigid, setting her from him as gently as he could. "No, Cecily."

His horses danced in place, eager to follow their companions, and he quieted them with a firm command.

"I beg your pardon," Cecily said, blushing and looking down at her hands. "I should not have done that." A moment later, she pulled the signet ring from her finger. "Here. Take this as a remembrance of an old friendship."

"Your ring? But isn't it something you had from Alec?"

She shook her head. "No, no. It is not a McInnes ring. Not at all. Please. I want you to take it."

In the end, for the sake of getting out of the *caravanserai* before the troops that awaited them could see them leaving, he accepted the ring, slipping it onto his smallest finger over his glove.

"Goodbye, Cecily. And good luck."

کمبل همه چیز برای عشق

James and his men left the *caravanserai* before dawn and were well into the desert before they saw any sign of pursuit and then only far behind and soon out of sight. They kept going. Turkmen horses had a smooth ground-eating gait they could keep up for hours, and James had no intention of stopping before they reached the mountains.

Riding gave him plenty of time to think over the encounters at the *caravanserai*. Had his father really expected him to tamely come to heel? No, probably not, hence the armed band outside the village. The Russian involvement worried him. The overland route to bypass the Ottomans was beginning to look like a bad idea. And Cecily. How likely was it that she arrived at such a remote location by coincidence? Had she somehow heard he was there? He couldn't fathom it. It wasn't as if they'd really known one another. She had been Eleanor's friend and years younger than him. Until he met her again, he hadn't thought of her in two decades. In truth, he hadn't thought of Eleanor, either, in years. Instead, his mind and heart were occupied by a very different lady.

کمبل همه چیز برای عشق

1779, Sarbisheh, Iran

"I have several pieces of unpleasant news," said Lady Emma Finstanley. She had sent the attendants and guards to the other side of the room so they could speak privately and was herself pouring black Persian coffee into delicate glasses.

The lady had been a surprise. When James and his party had

been captured and brought here to Sarbisheh, they had not
expected to find a Khan fascinated by all things English because his
own mother was an English lady.

James accepted the glass she passed to him and selected a sugar
cube to hold between his teeth to sweeten the liquid as he drank.
"Several pieces, my lady? Not something that will prevent your
visits, I hope."

One by one, the other hostages had been ransomed and
released, until James and his valet were the only prisoners left. Lady
Emma had taken to calling on him in the enclosed garden at the
base of the tower with her chief guard and several of her ladies to
chaperone. Her visits helped pass the time. Sometimes, she brought
her enchanting granddaughter with her, a slender girl who kept her
veil on in his presence and said little but not today. Today, Lady
Emma was clearly not here for casual gossip or remembrances of
England. He braced for whatever she had to disclose.

"We shall see," she said. "How high does your candle of love still
burn for Lady Eleanor, my dear boy?"

Lady Emma had been most sympathetic when James told his
tragic story. He had fallen in love with the daughter of an earl, and
what could be more suitable since he was the son of a duke? But
their fathers had forbidden the match and pressured Eleanor to
marry the Duke of Haverford instead, a *roué* of twice her age. James
found himself tied and delivered to a ship, with instructions to
deliver him as far from England as possible, and as he made his way
home again, he had been captured by the Khan.

"Do you still love her, James?" Lady Emma was leaning forward
over her cup, her eyes concerned.

"Of course," he replied, though when he tried to call to mind
the colour of her eyes or the shape of her lips or the dear sweet
scent of her, he struggled to bring the picture to full clarity.

"I am sorry. A letter has finally arrived from your father, and the
news is all bad." She put her glass down on the tray and folded her
hands in her lap.

He followed her example, taking a deep breath. "Give me the
worst of it, please, my lady."

She nodded, gravely. "The worst, then, and after something to perhaps mitigate it a little. Remember that, James. Your life is not over."

James waited for her to reach her point, resisting the urge to demand or implore.

"Swiftly, then. There will be no ransom. Your father has written to say you are dead to him. He also writes that the Lady Eleanor, having been told of your death, has obeyed her father and is now the Duchess of Haverford."

The moan James could not repress had several of the attendants turning to look. Yousef, his head guard, took a step toward him. He and James had become sparring partners, chess opponents, and friends in the eighteen months of waiting for the Duke of Winshire to pay for the return of his exiled son. He would probably be given the job of beheading the useless hostage, or was James to be handed over for castration?

Fear drove out the pain of his loss. Until today, he would have said he did not want to live without Eleanor. Apparently, he was wrong.

James tried to keep his voice calm as he put his trepidation into words. "Then I am of no further use to the Khan."

Lady Emma examined her nails. "As to that, I have spoken with my son." She lifted her light blue eyes, so admired in this Middle-Eastern land. "I have reminded him that you are a master of sword, unarmed fighting, and gunnery. In these troubled times, James, the Khan has need of loyal commanders to train and lead his troops, especially since he has a plan to send my Mahzad away. She will need a personal guard. I want that guard to be willing to do anything, anything at all, James, to keep her safe and deliver her to where she can be happy."

And that was how it began.

5

Pari-Daiza Vadi

"Have you confined your father to his rooms?" *Mamani* asked, a laugh bubbling in her voice.

Mahzad looked up from the report she was reading. "Not at all, *Mamani*. He took to his rooms because he is displeased. I merely posted a guard to make sure those he has managed to offend in the past three days do not further annoy him."

So far, he had upset the valley's military commander, its elders, her secretarial staff, and his own caravan guards. He could not seem to understand that he was no longer the Khan of Sarbisheh.

He was particularly offended that his slaves refused to obey him and blamed Mahzad for their defection. Quite properly, though it was by her husband's decree that no one within their *kagan* owned a slave, and that all slaves were made freedmen as soon as they entered within the borders of the valley. Mahzad had ordered her people to explain this to those who came with the caravan.

Mamani accepted the change with equanimity, offering her former slaves a wage if they would continue to work as her servants. Garshasp lost his temper and would have been left to make his own bed and fetch his own meals if Mahzad had not taken pity on him and sent some of the palace's menservants to see to his comfort.

The larger problem was unsolved, however.

According to Gurban's report, the soldiers at the gates refused to leave without Garshasp Khan. They had fetched cannon up from the plains but could not deploy the infernal machines in the narrow space that faced the gate and was well covered by the *serkerde's* riflemen and archers. On the other hand, the people of Pari-Daiza were locked in their valley, the back-door egress being suitable only for climbers. And their numbers were limited, even with the addition of the caravan guard, whose loyalty could not be relied on. If the Qajar forces were determined enough, they could draw on the resources of an entire army. Already, their attacks had left two men dead and another dozen wounded, though they had suffered heavier losses themselves.

Enough. She had read the report several times and had no more idea now than at the start about how to break the impasse.

The curtain over the door lifted to allow the valley's elders into the counsel room and then again to let Gurban and his deputy join them. The clerics were next, and everyone took their seats on cushions around the maps and diagrams spread out on a low table.

Gurban looked askance at *Mamani*.

"Mahroch *begum* is here at my request, Gurban," Mahzad said, "and I have also sent for Garshasp Khan. They must know why the Qajar are so determined. James has seen their day coming for some years and has been careful to maintain treaties with them." She was watching *Mamani* carefully as she spoke, but she turned her attention to her father as he entered the room, though she addressed the rest of her remark to the group at large. "For them to ignore these treaties in pursuit of a khan whose time has passed and who has abandoned his province to them… It needs further explanation."

"They are stubborn savages," Garshasp said.

"They want your head, *Padar*, and will not leave without it." Mahzad added dryly. "The rest of you is optional."

"You are an unnatural daughter and a deep disappointment to me," he said, sighing as he lowered himself to a pile of cushions.

"Very probably," she agreed and then looked around at her advisers, meeting the gaze of each one before she spoke again. "I am your *katan*," she reminded them. "Jakob *kagan* has said it, and so it is, but we rule by your mandate. It has been so since we came here."

"It has been so," said the headman gravely, and the others nodded.

"Do I, then, have the right to risk the valley and the people, for the sake of my father and grandmother, especially when they are keeping secrets from us? And yet, my dear people, I owe them honour and respect, as both the Bible and the Qur'an teach us. What am I to do?"

She spread her hands and let the silence build. No one seemed willing to be the first to speak. It was a trick James had taught her. Say nothing, and someone will fill the silence. Not any of her people, prewarned to stay quiet. Would her father or her grandmother be the first to fill the void?

It was Garshasp. "You would not give me to the Qajar," he stated, his voice booming in the chamber, as if volume could increase his confidence.

Mahzad said nothing, just tipping her head in question, but neither of her relatives spoke. How she wished James was here!

"My lady," Gurban said, "they say the khan has stolen something."

Mahzad kept her eyes on her father as she asked, "What do they claim the khan has, and why is it theirs and not his?"

"They would not say, my lady."

"Well, Padar? What do you have that they want?"

The khan smirked. "I will tell no one but your husband, the *kagan*."

Enough. If she could not have the counsel of the *kagan*, she would have the wisdom of the best minds left in the valley. "Well, my people? What are our next steps?"

کمبل همه چیز برای عشق

Caspian Sea Coast

Cecily carefully made her way through the *caravanserai* to meet the Turkmen woman who had promised to guide her. She needed to be well on her way before Gerry and Nikolai realised they had lost James Winderfield. The man's stubbornness had lost her the freedom and money she had been promised for her cooperation. Worse, Nikolai would take James's escape out on her, and Gerry would probably enjoy watching.

She was under no illusions about her fate at their hands. Her own bitter experience warned her. She had been abandoned in Lebanon when her husband and their baby son died, sold to a local dignitary as a concubine, and then passed on to another and then another in various parts of the Ottoman Empire.

At last, she found herself in Istanbul where her current master loaned her to the Russian Ambassador, who had been all sympathy at her tale. Or so she thought until she found he wanted to use her to scupper James's shipping plans by helping the agent sent to bring him back to England. Having failed, she would be sold again, and with every year that passed, her novelty value as an English woman depreciated further thanks to the aging of her body.

She would not tamely go back to that life, and she would fare no better if she struck out across Turkmenistan or Persia on her own.

No. She had only one choice—to go after James and persuade him to keep her. She knew he wanted her. She had seen the reaction of his body. She even honoured him for refusing to succumb to it. And if her own dire need did not drive her…

But what else could she do?

Besides, his marriage to the native woman was probably illegal and clearly unhappy. She would not be breaking anything that was not already dead. With eight children already, the woman would probably be grateful to have Cecily to distract her husband's fertile attentions. Eastern women saw these things differently.

Yes. She would follow James, and all would be well.

کمبل همه چیز برای عشق

Pari Daiza Vadi

A small army was camped at the gates into Pari Daiza, not
friends by the fact that the gates remained firmly closed and that
Gurban had snipers on the mountain.

"Thirteen tents," Peter observed. "They won't be at our front
door long, not with that number."

"They are between us and the gate now," Yousef pointed out.

"We won't be going in by the front door," James agreed.

They backed away, staying low until they were on the other side
of the slope, hidden from both the valley and the invaders, and then
plunged down the narrow trace of a path as quickly as could be
done in near silence.

Below, only their own people remained, the Atabai clan who
had been their escort into the mountains having taken most of the
horses, mules, and camels back down to the plains. Only the surest
footed horses and donkeys remained, and no eyes other than those
of their own people to see them hide the bulk of the packages they'd
brought back from their long travels.

"It'll be the secret way, my friends," James told those waiting.
"Plan to take only what you must. The rest will go into the caves."

For himself, James retrieved little. They could collect the
baggage once the problem at the gate was sorted, but he had
presents for Mahzad and the children. Those he wrapped for secu-
rity and strapped firmly to Melagush's saddle, packing it as tightly to
the horse's sides as he could.

The path home wound around the eastern side of the protective
mountain walls, climbing and dropping, never wide enough for
more than one man or one cautiously stepping horse. At times, it
seemed to disappear altogether, and they had to edge their way
across slopes toward the landmarks that James and Yousef had
carried in their heads since they first came this way thirteen years
earlier.

At last, Yousef, taking his turn in the lead, rounded a corner to
where the path ended altogether, or so it seemed. By the time James,
at the tail end of the small procession, arrived, only two were before
him, and one was even now leading his horse gingerly across the

slope to the right of the path then around the rocky bluff out of sight. The second to last man followed, and then James, into the long cave, sloping downward, that led under the mountains and into the valley.

He emerged onto the parade ground behind the citadel and to a welcoming committee. Gurban, good man, and a troop of his best men, relaxed now, chatting with the rest of his party but ready to defend the valley even against him, had he been coerced to showing enemies the secret way.

And here she came. Mahzad, running down from the citadel, outstripping her maids and even her older sons who raced each other, shouting and waving as they came.

Mahzad faltered on the edge of the parade ground, but by then, James was in motion, striding toward her, his arms wide in greeting.

In moments, she was in his arms.

6

___

Mahzad had only a few seconds in her husband's embrace, listening to the murmured endearments she'd longed for before the children arrived. The three older boys attached themselves to the couple, being hugged in their turn, and then Rachel and Rebecca threw themselves into the family huddle. Andrew and Ruth watched, uncertain, from the safety of their nursemaids.

The *kagan* was home, and now, all would be well.

All too soon, the children were sent back to the citadel, obedient to their father's command and buoyed by a promise of a family dinner with just them and their parents. "And presents, Papa?" Rachel asked. Mahzad scolded, but James allowed that yes, there might even be presents.

"Now, life of my heart," he said as the children and their servants trailed back up the steps to the citadel, "tell me about the trouble at our gates and what has brought it upon us."

Quickly, Mahzad and Gurban told him all that happened, breaking off frequently as yet another group of people came running to check that the arrivals were, indeed, their people and their *kagan*.

"So," James said, once he had the gist of it, "the Khan has a secret, which he will tell only to me. Very well. Let us give him the opportunity."

They did not have to look for the man. As they entered the palace, Garshasp Khan was waiting, wearing a huge smile.

"My son Jakob, you are come home. Welcome. Welcome. Peace be upon you."

Mahzad crushed her irritation at her father's arrogance, acting as if this were his own house and not hers and James's. James took the greeting with equanimity, returning the formal greeting. "Peace be upon you, Excellency. We are blessed that you have chosen to grace our house."

"You will say so." Garshasp chortled. "You will say so indeed. I have brought you a treasure, Jakob."

James said nothing more but led the way into a chamber off the main hall, turning everyone away except Mahzad, Gurban, and Garshasp.

James wasted no time, cutting straight to the point with Western directness. "I took from you a treasure, excellency, and for her sake you are always welcome here, but you have also brought trouble to my gates. I am told you have promised me an explanation."

"And you shall have it. I took it from its hiding place the moment I knew you were here. Look, my son. Look."

Mahzad leant forward to see the small gold item her father pulled from his robes. James plucked it from Garshasp's palm and held it up so that she and Gurban could see.

"A seal stamp?" Gurban asked.

"The inscription reads 'Abu Rahman ul Hafi," Mahzad said. She turned to look at her father aghast.

"Abu Rahman ul Hafi?" James closed his fingers over the seal, hiding it from view. "The saint whose shrine is in Asadiyeh?" He whistled low and long. "No wonder the Qajar are at my gates."

Garshasp smiled broadly. "A treasure, as I told you, and one you can use to buy the safety of my daughter and my grandsons."

Mahzad rounded on the old fool. "We were safe until you brought them on us."

The old man looked down his long nose at her. "Think you the

Qajar would leave any of my blood alive? No. The purge is underway even as we speak. And you, you ungrateful woman, are the last of my children. Your sons are the only hope of my line."

She would have retorted, but James cut through with quiet authority. "You will address Mahzad with respect, excellency. She is no longer merely your daughter. She is the *katan* of this valley, a position her merits won for her. Beyond that, she is, as you have pointed out, my wife and the mother of my sons and daughters."

"Daughters!" Garshasp growled. "Wait till your own are grown and then talk to me of daughters. Hah! I have given you the seal, Jakob. Use it as you will, and the rest of the goods I brought with me are for you and your sons, though half the value was in the slaves, which this wife of yours declared free. You will excuse me. This old man needs to rest." He turned and strode out, though his steps faltered as he passed through the doorway.

"Is he ill?" James asked.

"Not that I know," Mahzad answered, but perhaps he was. He had little appetite, spent much of his time asleep, and had needed to be carried back from the defensive walls yesterday, though he had claimed that was due to a touch of the sun.

Gurban looked thoughtful. "His ankles are swollen, Jakob *Beg*, and his breath comes fast, especially if he walks. My father was like that. He had the cough, too."

Gurban's father had died three years ago.

"His heart troubles him?" Mahzad wondered.

James frowned. "What does your grandmother say?"

"Nothing." Did he blame her for not noticing? "I will ask her, James."

James nodded and turned to his military commander. "Gurban, will you send a message to the commander of the Qajar troops asking for a meeting?" Then he smiled at Mahzad. "As for you and I, light of my world, let us go and give the children their presents."

Mahzad warmed at the endearments, tucking her arm into the elbow her husband offered her and thrilling at the warmth and strength of his muscles under her hand. "Life of my heart" and "light of my world" were common Persian expressions. They meant nothing, but her heart would not listen to the cautious warnings of her mind, not when James was home, his hand cupped over hers, his thigh brushing her hip as they walked.

کمبل همه چیز برای عشق

James resented every circumstance that kept him from his wife. Not, perhaps, the children. He was introduced to little Rosemary, who was a perfect miniature of her mother, and became reacquainted with the rest of his offspring as he fished through his pack of surprises for their presents.

"Look, Mama, a sailing boat like in the book!" Andrew ran across the room to show his mother, wildly waving the boat and narrowly missing his sister as he passed.

Mahzad took him up onto her lap and showed him how to hold it safely.

"I have a boat for each of you," James explained, looking up from showing young Jamie how to set the rudder on his perfect miniature of a *jahazi*, a broad-hulled trading *dhow*, "even Rosemary and little Ruth. When they are bigger, they will be able to race with you on your mother's pond." He met Mahzad's eyes. Her frown was belied by her dancing eyes. "With your mother's permission, of course."

"Mine is a brigantine," John boasted. "See Mama?"

He leaned on his mother's shoulder and began a discourse on the difference between gaff-rigged and square-rigged sails, accurate as far as James's recently-acquired knowledge went. He must have learned it from books, since he'd never seen a sail boat larger than the one in his hands or a body of water bigger than the pond in the valley when it flooded with the spring melt.

Jamie and Matthew abandoned their model boats when he handed over the cases holding their next presents. In moments, they were taking sword craft positions, balancing lightly on the balls of their feet, a scimitar in one hand, a rapier in the other.

"These are not toys, my sons," James warned. "Your mother and I judge you old enough to treat them with the respect they deserve and to learn how to handle them without danger to yourself or others."

"Except those who threaten our people, Papa," Jamie insisted.

"There is another case," Matthew observed.

Mahzad looked in alarm at John, who was too absorbed in his boat to notice.

James was quick to reassure her that he did not mean to set John to sword fighting with an edged weapon. Not yet. "It is for your Mama," James told Matthew.

He'd received the benison of his fierce warrior queen's smile when he had given Rebecca and Rachel good English yew bows in miniature and a quiver full of arrows each, but it was nothing to the glow that greeted her own sword case. The children, hugging their own gifts, stopped to watch her. Matthew let out a long sigh of pleasure as Mahzad lifted the sheathed sword in two hands.

"Toledo made," James said. It was a Western-styled small sword, like the ones he'd taught her with but in the best steel in Europe, perhaps the world.

She slid the blade partway from the scabbard, and when her eyes met his, the heat in them made him wish his much-loved offspring at the other end of the palace. He smiled her a promise for later and turned back to passing out children's books in English that he'd purchased in Siricusa, in Sicily.

He'd left the Christmas presents outside the valley to be brought in after they'd dealt with the Qajar troops. If Mahzad loved her blade, she would adore the pistols that were still packed in the abandoned luggage.

He was smiling at the thought when the messenger arrived.

"*Begum*, you must come at once. The Khan has taken ill."

کمبل همه چیز برای عشق

The Khan was dying but perhaps not tonight, said the doctor from the village. Mahzad and her grandmother insisted on attending him themselves, one either side of the bed. James, since he could not take Mahzad to bed as he wanted, spent the rest of the afternoon picking up the reins of government. Mahzad had done an exceptional job, as always, but she could relax now he was back to take over.

In between meetings, he checked on his father-in-law. The man was sleeping, his mother watching over him.

"Is Mahzad—" James began, but Mahroch *begum* interrupted.

"Mahzad has gone to feed Rosemary and to kiss the children goodnight. She said she would be back soon."

James suppressed a yawn. Two days and a night in the saddle, followed by the climb and then an eventful afternoon left him longing for his bed, but he would find energy if he could persuade his wife to join him.

He'd head for the nursery and say his own goodnights. He could escort his wife back to her father's bedside. He could, perhaps, steal a kiss somewhere along the way.

Before he could leave, Garshasp called out. "Is that Jakob? Jakob, are you there?"

"Yes, excellency," he agreed, taking the seat Mahzad had vacated.

"I am dying, Jakob." The old man took the hand James laid on the bed and gripped it tight in his own.

"Rest, excellency. You have the best of care."

"I am dying. The doctors in Sarbisheh said I would be dead within a year, and that was six months ago. Who will mourn me? Who will keep my memory alive in the land of the living? My sons are gone, all of them. Wasted." He glanced at his mother and then turned his eyes back to James. "I should have given them to my mother to raise. Their own mothers made arrogant fools out of them. If Mahzad had been a boy… Ah, what an heir she would have been."

He rambled on for a while, praising Mahzad for her wisdom and courage, as well as her four sons, berating her for abandoning the marriage her father had planned, complaining about his disappointment in his other children. James listened as patiently as he could, trapped by the hand hold he was reluctant to break.

In the end, Mahzad arrived back just as Garshasp drifted back off to sleep. James departed to see the children on his own, his opportunity for a few minutes with his wife lost. He'd join her again, but first, he'd snatch a small nap. In his own chambers, he lay down on his bed, still fully dressed. The next thing he knew, it was morning.

کمبل همه چیز برای عشق

The Khan slept deeply, waking when the doctor arrived to examine him the following morning. "He is much recovered since last night, my *katan*," the doctor told Mahzad. "He has survived this spasm. He could have another at any time, but he is out of danger until then."

His visit had made Mahzad late for her daily meeting with the valley's government, but she had sent a message explaining the delay and asking them to wait. She had half thought James might come to support her, but she had not seen him since he left to visit the children the night before.

She paused to compose herself as she came through the curtained door into the audience chamber. Despite his tender words and his physical presence, James seemed as far away as ever. How were they to bridge the gap?

From beyond the pierced wooden screen that hid her entrance, she heard sounds of people making their farewells, and she leaned forward to peer through the cutouts. The meeting was over? It certainly seemed so, as first one and then another of the village councillors made their obeisance to James and left. Had she and her work as their *katan* been so easily dismissed? Her father's disregard had been expected, but this cut her to the soul.

No. She would not look at it so. James probably thought he was helping by freeing her to look after her father. She was about to step out from behind the screen when Gurban arrived, apologising for being late.

Mahzad narrowed her eyes at the cloaked figure that one of his lieutenants held at the door while James and Gurban moved out of his earshot and closer to the screen.

"They have sent down to their base camp for their commander, *Beg*."

What was wrong with Gurban? He stood straight and formal, his face impassive. And the simple honourific, "*beg*" or "lord" as the English would say. Most of his senior advisors and warriors, Gurban among them, called their *kagan* "James" at his request, except in the presence of their juniors.

James didn't comment, but Mahzad was sure he noticed. He, too, was examining the cloaked figure. "He will agree to a meeting, I imagine. What else have you brought me, Gurban?"

"An act of good will, the Qajar siege commander called it." Gurban's voice was stiff with disdain. "They apparently captured your woman on her way to rejoin you."

James swore, a couple of English epithets he used only rarely, and took three strides toward the woman at the door. "Cecily, just what do you think you are playing at?"

Mahzad waited to hear no more, turning and slipping out of the door, grateful she had brought none of her ladies with her to witness her humiliation.

Though if her husband had brought his mistress here to install her under this roof, more humiliation was unavoidable.

7

———

S now was falling in the paradise garden, preventing Mahzad from taking the calming walk she needed. She ordered the shutters closed in the great common room where the ladies of the house gathered to socialise but those in her own chambers left open, the stark lines of the garden in its winter state fitting her bleak mood.

"Mahzad?" It was James, leaning against her door jamb, frowning at her. "Your mother said you were in here. I thought you would be with your father."

Mahzad shrugged one shoulder only, a minuscule lift and drop. "He is sleeping. The doctor says he is recovering from this attack but could have another at any time."

Her husband's frown deepened, the vertical crease between his brows deepening. "I know. I spoke to him. I am sorry, Mahzad. It must distress you."

Mahzad turned back to the window. "I have not seen him in fifteen years, not since he sent me to the other side of the world to be one wife among many in a foreign land, but still, I remember that I was once his treasure."

Yes, she hated seeing the once-powerful man so shriveled and ill, and she grieved for the loss of what they once had, but if James thought her distress due to her father, he was a blind fool.

"I am sorry," James repeated. "And sorry to add further to your burdens, but…" He trailed off, and from the corner of her eye, Mahzad saw him spread his hands and shrug. "I have someone to introduce to you. Will you come out and meet her?"

Mahzad whirled at that and stalked toward him. "You do not expect me to find room for your mistress in my house, surely?"

James took a step toward her, his quiet hiss at odds with his blazing eyes. "Cecily is not my mistress, and you do neither me nor yourself any credit in making such an accusation."

"Hah!" Mahzad's bark was nothing like a laugh. "Then what is she doing here? This female who claims to be your woman and follows you home?"

James took a deep breath, visibly struggling for calm. "She is an English lady and an old friend. You must see I cannot abandon her when she asks me for help."

Mahzad fought back several scorching responses. If James could be dignified, she could also. "Very well. Present her to me."

"Mahzad."

James never addressed her with that voice of command, delivered sternly and without room for debate. Putting on the *kagan*, he called it. *But with me? Has it come to this?*

"Mahzad, she must stay here, under your wing. Half the citadel is jumping to the wrong conclusion about her, and I fear for her safety."

Mahzad did not trust herself to speak but just brushed past James, holding herself so she touched him as little as possible.

The woman, uncloaked now, waited in the main chamber, standing alone a few feet into the room. The women of the citadel gathered in groups around her, all talking, none of them approaching. She looked older than Mahzad by several years but was still attractive, especially to those who preferred the blonde hair and blue eyes of the northerners. She would be a valuable courtesan, at least for a few more years.

She won Mahzad's reluctant respect with the calm nonchalance she displayed in the face of the room's barely-veiled hostility. Or perhaps she trusted James to save her? Did she think to replace Mahzad as ruler of the women's realm?

Mahzad had not played these women's games in fifteen years, but the lessons of her youth were easily at hand. She approached her rival with her hand extended in the Western fashion.

"Cecily, is it? My husband tells me he has offered to help you for the sake of an old friendship. For his sake, I must also stand as your friend. I am Mahzad, *katan* of this *kaganate* and ruler of this *zenana*. Peace be upon you, and all who come here in goodwill."

کمبل همه چیز برای عشق

James left Cecily with the women, pleased to wash his hands of her, at least for a while. Didn't he have enough to deal with? Armies at his gate. A wife who was clearly peeved with him about something, though he'd hardly been home long enough to offend her. A dying father-in-law. And now the whole palace seemed to have made up its mind that Cecily was his mistress. Even Mahzad, who should know him well enough to trust him.

Cecily was not helping, prattling on to Mahzad about how close she and James had been in London. "…a long, long time ago, my lady. I hate to think of the many years that have passed. You can only imagine how thrilled I was that he recognised me straight away and was willing to rekindle our old friendship."

James could tell some of Mahzad's ladies put the worst possible construction on Cecily's words, but the stupid female kept on, and Mahzad seemed to be encouraging her, asking her innocent-seeming questions about her travels.

James excused himself, saying he'd promised to take the saint's seal down to the mosque, which would be its temporary home until he could send it back to where it belonged.

A pleasant visit with the *mojtahed* and his friend the priest, followed by the promised sword craft lesson with his two eldest boys left him in a more cheerful frame of mind, which improved still further with a message from the siege, setting a meeting for the following day.

Back in his chambers, Peter was going on about crickets, something about one in the garden making an unseasonable racket just before Cecily McInnes had arrived.

"The cricket knew," Peter pronounced.

James didn't bother to ask what the cricket knew, but just sent Peter with a message to Mahzad, inviting her to join him for a private dinner. The message didn't need to say "and bed after." Mahzad would guess.

Peter returned with a note and a glum face.

"Your humble servant begs leave to be excused, most excellent lord," James read. "Your obedient wife, Mahzad."

Like hell! He brushed Peter aside and strode through the halls, the people he passed taking one look at his face and getting out of his way.

The guards on the door to the *zenana* stepped aside and let him through without a challenge. Mahzad wasn't in the central room. She wasn't in her chambers, either. He emerged back into the great room, casting an eye around the ladies who were there. Cecily, who was sitting with Mahroch, made as if to get up.

Mahroch put out a hand to stop her. "Sit. You have caused enough trouble."

James directed his glare at Mahroch, but the old woman was not discomposed in the slightest. She needed the help of a maid to rise, but she waved the girl off and walked with much of her old grace toward Mahzad's chambers.

"Come, Lord James. You and I need to talk."

"I need to see my wife." He snarled.

"Not before we have talked."

He followed her, of course, but his irritation was rising by the minute.

She deflated him by rounding on him as soon as they were in private. "James, I always thought you to be an intelligent man and one with enough sense to see what was in front of his nose, but I am disappointed in you."

Attack being the best form of defence, he answered hotly, "Don't tell me that you believe these scurrilous rumours about Mrs. McInnes. She is not my mistress. Not that I owe you or anyone else an explanation."

Mahroch lifted an elegantly plucked eyebrow. "Not even my granddaughter?"

"Mahzad should know I would never dishonour her." James relieved some of his tension by striding swiftly across the room and then back again. "Yes, and the rest of the citadel, too. It is a ridiculous conclusion to jump to. Insulting to me and to Mrs. McInnes. I can understand the Qajar commander but my own people?" His temper, barely in check when he'd arrived, was now at boiling point.

Mahroch was neither intimidated nor impressed. "Your own people, including your wife, would have been less inclined to make assumptions about your relationship with Cecily McInnes had she not been at pains to give the impression that you and she are lovers."

"No." That couldn't be true. "She didn't, did she? But why?"

The old woman dismissed his question with an elegant wave of one hand. "She had her reasons, and I am somewhat in sympathy with her, though I have put a stop to her mischief." She bent forward, meeting his glare with her own. "But it remains for you to undo the damage that she—and you, I might add—have done."

"What have I done?" James protested. "I have done nothing!"

"You will have to discuss that with my granddaughter, James," Mahroch replied sharply. Her voice dried as she continued. "I suggest you spend at least part of the time listening. You will find her at the archery butts, I imagine. When she left here, she felt like killing something. Oh, and just a small hint. It would not harm your masculine essence to tell her how you feel about her."

What was that supposed to mean? As James stalked through the citadel and down into the cellars, he tried to think about Mahroch's last remark, but the injustice of the accusations against him kept shouldering out other considerations. Not least because, for a fraction of a moment back at the *caravanserai* when Cecily had offered herself, temptation had reared its serpently head. Only physically and he dismissed it, of course. He should be receiving credit for that, not suspicion and a cold shoulder for thoughts he'd never had and actions he'd not taken.

Cecily's treachery didn't bother him as much as Mahzad's willingness to believe the lying woman. Felt like killing something, did she? James felt like spanking someone, and he blamed Mahzad for that entirely. He'd never raised his hand in anger to a woman in his life, especially not Mahzad, who had been his equal and his partner since the day they had escaped her father's caravan.

Mahzad had posted a man at the doors to the range to prevent anyone else entering.

"Try to stop me," James invited, and the guard wisely stepped to one side.

Inside, every lamp was lighted, but even so, the butts wavered in and out of shadows. Not that Mahzad was fooled for a moment. Arrow after arrow slammed into the centre of each target as she drew and shot, drew and shot, drew and shot, a dozen arrows at a time and then only seconds to reach for the next dozen and begin again.

"I am not having, nor have I had, an affair with Cecily McInnes," James said loudly and was pleased when her aim faltered slightly, the next two arrows striking outside the inner circle. "I have slept with no one but you since I met you, wife, and I am insulted you should think otherwise."

Mahzad finished firing the arrows in her hand then put her bow and quiver carefully on the table beside her before turning to face him.

"I do not think it. The woman is a liar." She lifted her chin, her eyes blazing. "But I am insulted that you would bring someone to make such claims under my roof. Did you intend to make me a laughing stock in front of my ladies and my maids?"

"Of course not," he growled. "I had no idea that she was saying such things."

Mahzad spat like an angry cat. "Hah. And if you had? Would you have turned her back out the gate? Left her to the Qajar? No, of course not. Not an Englishwoman. Not a friend of dear Eleanor."

"No. No, I would not have left her to her fate, even if she deserves it." James thumped one fist into his hand. Women were so unreasonable. "And what has Eleanor to do with it? Mahzad, you cannot possibly be jealous of Eleanor. I haven't seen her in twenty years. She is married. I am married and happily I thought." Just like that, some of his anger seeped away, drowned in sorrow.

Mahzad, though, was just getting started. "Happily? When you spend as much time as you can away from me? What am I to you, James? Tell me the truth."

What sort of a question is that?

"You are my wife. The mother of my children. You know this."

"Yes." Her voice was sad, and as she lifted her chin, he thought he caught a gleam of tears in her eyes. "As I thought. You do your duty."

"No!" What was wrong with her? "That's not what I meant. What is the matter, Mahzad? Is it the baby?"

The tears disappeared, and she flared into rage again. "What is the matter with me? What is the matter with you! Walking back in after seven months—seven months, James—and ignoring everything I have done. How could you hold this morning's meeting without me? I sent a message to say I would be there soon and arrived to find you dismissing the meeting and greeting that whore. I beg your pardon. Let me rephrase that. Greeting that 'dear friend from your younger days.'"

"What?" He ignored the provocation of her description of Cecily. She was offended that he held the meeting without her? "I thought to take a burden off you when your father was so ill. I meant no insult, Mahzad. You should know that."

"How?" she demanded. "By mindreading? I have lost my magic abilities, oh inscrutable one. My genie is in retirement." She turned away, her voice dropping. "I have no idea why you do the things you do, except that I know I am a burden to you. I am sorry to inconvenience you and your father by continuing to exist."

Exasperating female. Would she stick to the point?

"What the devil do you mean now? What has my father got to do with it?"

"He wants you to come back to England," Mahzad accused. "Your 'oh so dear' Cecily told me, and Peter and Yousef confirmed it." She sniffed and tossed her head. "You will not go because I am an embarrassment to you."

"Like hell you are," James snapped. "Neither of them said that, and if they did, it isn't true."

She was avoiding his eyes, bending over her weapons, putting the arrows neatly away into the quiver and unstringing the bow. "They said you refused to go and that you told your father's men that you would not leave your wife." She whirled back to face him, snarling in her turn. "I say little difference if you did, since you are never here anyway and spend no time with me when you are."

James was reeling from her dozen blows, some of which had got completely under his guard, but this last remark matched so closely to his own feelings about Mahzad that he struck back.

"You're the one who is always busy and who never has time for me. You are too busy being *katan* and mother and friend to everyone in the valley. You've made it more than clear you don't need me, and you don't want me around." He took a step closer toward her, crowding her against the table. "But this is *my* valley. They are *my* children. You are *my* wife. It's about time you remembered that."

He seized her and forced his mouth down on hers, intending a punishing kiss that overwhelmed her defences and reminded her he was master in this area as in others, but she met his force with her own passion, softening under his invasion, molding her body to his as she clutched his head to pull him closer. His original intent forgotten, he poured all his longing into the kiss, trying to communicate his love and his frustration, losing himself in the touch and smell and sound of this one woman who was to him above all others.

Until she broke the kiss and shoved him away. "I cannot believe you blame me for all this," she said. "Just like a man."

And she stalked away, leaving him alone.

8

Mahzad had taken refuge in one of the unused rooms at the top of a tower. Patma knew where she was if she was needed and knew better than to tell anyone except in an emergency. Mahzad considered over and over again the words she'd exchanged with James, especially those she'd heard as she flounced from the room.

His voice, quietly grieving, repeated in her mind. "Mahzad, what has happened to us? I thought we loved one another."

Loved. As in once upon a time? As if he had loved her once and did no longer? Or did he think she had stopped loving him? He was wrong about that. The pain she felt at the distance between them, the pain that fuelled her anger, was directly proportional to the love she bore him.

The thought gave her pause. James was angry, angrier with her than she'd ever seen him. What fuelled his anger?

She had lit the brazier when she came up here, but the little fuel in its chamber was now charred ash, and the cold was seeping into her bones, even through her fur robe. She needed to return to the world below. Her children would be missing her, and her ladies would be concerned about her.

At the foot of the second flight of steps, a guard waited, studiously looking away as if she were invisible to him. She wished him a good evening and continued down to the gallery that led to the women's wing of the palace. A dozen steps toward her own realm and she stopped. She had to know. Was James angry because he loved her and feared his love had been spurned?

She whirled, disconcerting the guard from the tower, who had been following her and now tried to blend into the wall hangings. She had no time for him, turning into the hall that held the *kagan's* chambers.

The door was open and unguarded.

Mahzad fixed her guard with a stern stare. "You can stop following me now. Tell Gurban or Patma or whoever set you to the task that you saw me to my husband's rooms."

Inside, she quietly closed the door then followed the sound of voices to the main sitting room of the suite, her temper rising again as she identified the voice of the Englishwoman.

"Very well. You won't go back to England. I cannot understand how you could prefer this barbarous place to our homeland, but clearly, you will not be persuaded, but, James, will you not let me stay? I will do anything…"

Mahzad took two steps backward, not wanting to hear the woman seducing her husband. No. She would not be such a coward. She stepped forward again and was rewarded by the sound of her husband's voice, taut with distaste.

"Enough, Cecily. You have made your proposition quite clear. Yes, and lied about our relationship to my household. I am not in the market for the services you offer. As I told you before, I am a married man, and I keep my vows."

"But you cannot refuse me," Cecily argued, sounding bewildered. "The ring, it is the power of the ring to reunite lovers. Alec always said it was the ring that brought us together. When he lay dying, he said the ring would take me home. I gave you the ring, and you have to help me."

"To reunite lovers, is it?" James said. "Then it has done its job because it has brought me home to the woman I love. My wife."

"You said you were content." Cecily sounded disappointed. "You said nothing of love."

"True, and I should have," James agreed. "But to her, not to you. She is the life of my heart and the light of my life."

"And if she does not love you?" Cecily asked.

Almost Mahzad interrupted, but she yearned to know his response and kept still.

James was silent for a moment, and when he replied, his voice was warm with a smile. "Then I shall love her enough for us both and spend my life trying to be worthy of her."

Cecily gave a short laugh. "You had best talk to her then, fool of a man, for anyone with eyes can see you are 'the life of her heart and the light of her life.' I have wasted my time. I wish you well, James. I really do."

"*Mamani* told me a little of your story, Mrs. McInnes," Mahzad said as she entered the room, startling them both. "I will discuss your situation with my husband, and we shall agree on a way to help you. At the moment, however, James and I need to be alone."

Cecily swept an obeisance in the Eastern style. "You are generous, *begum*."

James, his heart in his eyes, did not look away from Mahzad as Cecily passed her and left the room and—Mahzad leaned backwards to check—the suite.

"I love you," James said when she turned back toward him.

"That occurred to me when I started to wonder why you were so angry," Mahzad said, staying where she was.

"You were angry too," he pointed out.

She nodded. "I was."

"Say the words. Say the words, Mahzad, and put me out of my misery."

She took a step toward him. "I love you, James." Another step. "You are an annoying…" Another step. "…frustrating, arrogant man…" A final step, into his arms, avoiding his seeking mouth so she could finish what she had to say. "…and I love you more than life itself."

He would wait no longer, but she was as impatient as him, and the important words had been said. Actions now were more welcome. There would be time enough for more words later.

کمبل همه چیز برای عشق

The negotiation with the Qajar had been straightforward enough, and the day before Christmas, the siege ended, and the troops set off for lower lands, taking with them the seal, a large gift that included two fine horses fully caparisoned in fine Turkmen harnesses, a small herd of their mountain sheep, and Cecily McInnes.

Cecily embraced Mahroch, who had first persuaded her to tell her story and then Mahzad. She looked at James and decided against offering him a kiss in farewell.

Quite right, too. The woman had been trouble enough. James had arranged her travel to East India Company residency at Bushehr on the Persian Gulf, had paid for passage from there to England, and had given her funds that should keep her in comfort once she arrived.

Mostly, he said to Mahzad, because he wanted her out of his *kaganate.* Mahzad just smiled. Cecily's story had won Mahzad's sympathy and that of most of the women and many of the men, including his own, though he should still be annoyed at her deceit. Would be, too, if he were not so happy.

Cecily mounted into the saddle on the camel that would carry her down the mountain, and the animal stood. They watched as the long train of soldiers and animals began winding around the trail out of the basin before the gates.

"All will be well now, my lord," Peter said happily. "We met the sheep coming toward us as we rode down to the gates, and that is good luck." At that moment, a white splash appeared on his sleeve, a present from a passing bird. "Even more good luck!" Peter cried, delighted, ignoring the laughter of Gurban's soldiers.

James nudged Melagush, who bounded ahead to prance beside Mahzad's mare, showing off his paces.

"What have you planned for the rest of the day?" Mahzad

asked. "The children are taking advantage of the lull in the weather to have a boat race."

"We could go and watch," James agreed. With the crisis over and the winter setting in, few would bother the valley until Spring. He and Mahzad could relax and enjoy their family… and one another. "Or we could tend to some of our unfinished business."

Mahzad thought about that, her lips pushed out in an adorable pout he would have kissed if not for embarrassing his wife in front of her grandmother, her ladies, and his warriors.

"We have a number of items still to count off, do we not?" she mused. "One hundred and ninety-seven by my calculation."

James could not hold in his bark of laughter. Dear heavens, he loved this woman. They had spent the night of their reunion making love, cuddling, and exploring the roots of the distance they had allowed to grow between them. In the morning, when she had commented on the number of times they had joined, he'd reminded her they were starting from a deficit, since he had been absent for two-hundred and thirteen days. "Then you owe me two-hundred and eight more times, my lord," she had quipped in response. He hadn't realised she'd been keeping count ever since.

He offered her his arm to escort her to her horse. "Then by all means, let us see if we can manage to reduce the count," he agreed.

If the grins of their court hinted at a better understanding than was entirely comfortable, James didn't care. He had followed a star like the Persian wise men of old, and it had brought him home.

THE END

GLOSSARY OF NON-ENGLISH TERMS

beg: (Turkic/Persian) higher official; prince or lord

begum: (Turkic/Persian) the female equivalent of beg; princess or lady

caravanserai: (Persian) a roadside inn

charar bāgh: (Persian) a four-part garden; the layout is based on the four gardens of Paradise mentioned in the Qur'an and has four smaller parts divided by walkways or water

kagan: (Turkmen) ruler

kaganate: (Turkmen) kingdom

katan: (Turkmen) consort of the ruler

khan: (Turkic/Persian) ruler

mamani: (Persian) grandma

mojtahed: (Persian) a specialist in religious law

padar: (Persian) father

Pari-Daiza: (Persian) enclosed garden, the term first used for the notion of paradise

qal'a: (Persian) citadel

seraglio: (Turkish) the women's apartments in an Ottoman palace

serkerde: (Persian) military commander

zenana: (Persian) the women's apartments in an Iranian household

PART II

PARADISE LOST

The Duchess of Haverford has built a fulfilling and happy life centred on her children and her charities. She never forgets the man she once loved; the man she was prevented from wedding, but she no longer grieves him.

His return from Central Asia after thirty-five years has her considering those memories and others. Looking back lets her see how far she has come.

JUDE KNIGHT
Paradise Lost
A collection of vignettes prequelling The Children of the Mountain King
THE DUCHESS ALONE

To my newsletter subscribers, whose support helps to keep me writing. Thank you for reading my stories. Thank you for emailing me with your thoughts. I hope you enjoy this little book about Eleanor.

Haverford House, London, March 1812

The Duke of Haverford slammed the door on his way out, but it wasn't his temper that left his duchess trembling in her chair, her limbs so weak she could do nothing but sit, her chest hurting as she tried to force shallow breaths in and out. She had grown so used to his tantrums that she barely noticed.

"Your Grace?" Her secretary held out a hand as if to touch her then drew it back. The poor girl — a distant cousin just arrived from Berkshire — was as white as parchment. "Your Grace? Can I get you something? Can I pour you a pot of tea?"

Brandy would be welcome. A slight touch of amusement at Millicent's reaction to such a request helped soothe Eleanor's perturbation. "I should like to be alone, Millicent," she managed to say. A lifetime of pretending to be calm and dignified through grief, anger, fear, and desperate sorrow came to her rescue. "Can you please send a note to Lady Carew to ask her to hold me excused today? Ask her if tomorrow afternoon would be acceptable."

Once the girl left the room, casting an anxious glance over her shoulder, Eleanor stood and crossed to her desk, stopping before the mantel when her reflection caught her eye. If Millicent had been pale, Eleanor was worse — so white that dark patches showed under her eyes, eyes in which the pupil had almost swamped the iris.

It was the shock. Perhaps she would have that cup of tea before she fetched the box.

She poured it, and then added a spoonful of sugar. Two spoonfuls. She normally took her tea unsweetened, with just a slice of lemon, but hot sweet tea was effective in cases of shock, was it not?

With the cup set on the table by the chair, she spent a few minutes moving panels of wood in her escritoire, until the secret compartment at the back opened. It was large enough to contain boxes of various sizes, several small stacks of paper tied with ribbon into a bundle, and a dozen cloth bags.

She had to move some of the contents out of the way to reach what she wanted. The first of the boxes to be hidden in what she called her memory cabinet. She hadn't taken this one out since the afternoon of the day Grace and Georgie had told her — oh, some 15 years ago — that James still lived.

James had returned to England.

Haverford could shout as much as he liked about Winshire's heir being an imposter, about all the world knowing that the youngest son of the family had died in Persia three decades ago and more. But Eleanor had known almost as soon as Winshire's daughter and daughter-in-law knew that James still lived. Of course, he would come home now, when Winshire's other heirs had died. She should have expected it. Why had she not expected it?

Words from Haverford's rant came back to her as she sipped her tea and looked through the few treasures she had kept all these years, sacred to the memory of their doomed courtship. *Winshire says the man is his son.* The ribbon she wore in her hair the first time they danced. *He lies, of course.* A dried rose from a bouquet he had sent her. *The man has a pack of half-breeds that he claims are his children.* Several notes and two precious letters, including the one in which he asked her to elope. *Barbarians as Dukes of Winshire? Over my dead body!* A handkerchief he'd given her to dry her eyes when she cried while telling him that they must wait; that her father would come around. *Better to see the title in the hands of that idiot Wesley Winderfield than handed over to some cloth head.*

She had kept several brief notes about nothing in particular. 'I saw these and thought of you', on a card with a bouquet of sweet spring flowers. 'Save me a dance at the Mitford's tonight?' 'I saw you in the Park. You rode like a goddess.' They did not have to be signed. They were all from James, and short because they had been passed to her in secret.

She cradled the rose, fragile and faded. *I remember.*

کمبل همه چیز برای عشق

The garden of Creydon House, 1777

Lady Eleanor Creydon traced the words in the water that puddled on the stone rim of the fountain. "Lady James Winderfield." Her lips curved in a tremulous smile. The man she loved was asking her father for her hand, and would soon come to ask her.

"I have made an appointment to meet your father tomorrow," he had whispered in her ear last night as they promenaded down the centre of the double line of dancers. Then, as they passed one another, a few moments later, "You know what I want to ask him, my darling."

She circled the girl at the head of the ladies' line, barely aware of the other people in the room, conscious only of James and the words that set her heart thumping. Only years of practice kept her moving gracefully back around to meet James again, her arm stretched high, her hand ready for his brief clasp and her ears for another burst of whispered words.

"It is what you want?"

Looking up, she nodded, and the anxiety cleared from his eyes as they met hers. How could he be unsure of her? She had no further opportunity to reassure him. They had to part and dance down the outside of their respective lines, and the music drew to a close before they could speak again.

Her mother had been waiting, and hurried her away. The Earl of Farnmouth, her father, had decided it was time to leave the ball.

Eleanor had lain awake in the night, thinking that tomorrow would never come, but at last the sun had come up, and the interminable morning had passed.

James was with her father now, shut in the earl's study. Soon, surely, the earl would send him out into the garden. The answer would be yes, of course. As the daughter of an earl, she knew her worth, but James was third son of a duke; a duke, furthermore who was a friend of her father.

Eleanor cast a glance at the house and frowned slightly. Her father would say yes. Of course, he would. Only last week, he had interrupted her dinner with her mother to announce that he expected a very eligible offer for Eleanor's hand. "I am pleased with your daughter, countess," he had told her mother. "Betrothed only two months after her debut. You are to be congratulated, madam."

He had not spoken to Eleanor, but he seldom did, nor had he given a name. Who could it be but James? James was her most ardent suitor. Indeed, since the rapscallion son of the Duke of Winshire had made her the object of his devotion, the rest of her court had fallen away. They had been callow boys, in any case, standing up with her because of childhood friendship or because she had become fashionable.

James was a man, not a boy — twenty-four years to her seventeen. He was unbelievably handsome, charming, clever, funny, and dearer to her than anyone she had ever known, even her older sister. And he had chosen her! She clapped her hands and spun in a circle, unable to contain her delight.

Soon he would come. She composed herself on the stone bench opposite the path by which he would enter the garden. How would he propose? On one knee? Sitting beside her? The thought had her up on her feet again, too excited to stay still, peering down the path.

"Eleanor!" It was a hiss just a hairsbreadth above a whisper.

She spun around. James had come from the other direction. Well, no matter. She hurried towards him; her hands outstretched.

He scowled, his eyes blazing in a white face. "James? What is the matter?"

He clasped her hands and pulled her after him into the shadows of the yew walk, where he wrapped his arms around her and rested his chin on her hair. "Eleanor, I love you. I love you more than life itself. You believe me, do you not?"

Eleanor pulled away, but only enough to peer into his eyes. "James? What did my father say?"

James groaned.

"James, you are frightening me. Did he say we must wait?"

"Eleanor, he says that he has given your hand to the Duke of Haverford," James blurted.

Eleanor's breath stopped, and the blood surged in her ears as her heart pounded. Her sight grew dark at the edges, and the enormous yew hedges swayed towards her as if to batter her into the ground. By force of will, she fought off her faintness. "But… but he is old," she stammered, "and a wicked libertine, and cold as ice." She stamped her foot. "I don't want him, James. I love you. I love you, James."

"Shush, my love," James begged. "We must be quiet. Farnmouth told me I could not see you again, but I had to, Eleanor. I'll find a way. I promise. You love me, and I love you. I will ask my father to help. He is friends with yours. Surely Winshire can persuade the earl."

"Yes!" Eleanor's heart gave another enormous thump, this time with relief. "We will be together?" she asked.

"We will marry," James promised. He bent his head and his lips touched hers. It was a gentle, reverent salute, but Eleanor pressed closer and the kiss changed, James's lips still soft, but questing, moving, devouring. His tongue pressed the seam of her mouth and swept inside when she gasped. Again, the darkness hovered, but this time it was a welcoming warmth, a giving and taking of sensation, a merging of selves so that Eleanor no longer knew who sighed and who moaned, or how long they stayed intertwined.

The whistling of a gardener brought them back to themselves.

"I must go," James told her. "Stay strong, my love. We are meant to be together, and I will find a way."

"We are meant to be together," she agreed.

کمبل همه چیز برای عشق

Haverford House, London, March 1812

If she had said 'yes', what would have happened? He had a curricle in the mews. They could have left that night, straight from the garden where they'd slipped out for a private conversation. Haverford would not have assaulted her on her way back inside. James would not have challenged him to a duel, wounded him, and been exiled a step ahead of the constable.

Eleanor carefully replaced the rose and took out the letter her maid had brought her the afternoon after Haverford's horrifying assault had been followed by the announcement of her betrothal. The maid had hidden it under the tray cloth when delivering her breakfast so that the footmen who guarded her bedroom door didn't see it.

My dearest, dearest love

My father is in it, too. He says that Haverford is to have you, as soon as he has recovered from his wounds.

I wish I had never challenged the duke, or that I had shot to kill. I meant only to defend your honour; to show he could not speak of you as if you were his possession. Even a husband should hesitate to show such disrespect to the woman he has promised to cherish above all others, and so I told him. 'You are not even her betrothed,' I told him, 'and the last man on earth to deserve her'. I am very sorry, Eleanor. I lost my temper, when I should have been thinking of the best way to press my case with your father.

Now, the devil is in it, my father insists that I must flee the country. He says Haverford will have me arrested for shooting him, and Father won't lift a finger to stop him.

Come with me, Eleanor. The ship my father has organised leaves in two days, but I have a friend who can get me away tomorrow night. I promise I can look after you. I've sold the little estate my mother left me, so I have funds. We will go to the Continent. I can find work, I know I can, and we will be together.

I know it won't be what you are used to or what you deserve, but I love you, and you love me. Is that not worth fleeing for?

Meet me by the oak near the back gate of your garden as soon as the house is quiet tomorrow evening. I will be there. We have to be on the ship in time to sail with the dawn, and by the time your household wakes, we shall be gone down the river, and out to sea.

Come with me, my love.

Yours forever

James

Her father's voice, in her memory. *I'm not throwing you away on a third son, Eleanor Creydon. Winderfield is a fribble; a useless pup. Haverford wants you, and I've accepted him. Forget Winderfield.*

The letter was yellowed with time, and Eleanor, too, had faded with age. But she had not forgotten. She would never forget.

Had she been brave enough or clever enough to break out of her room and evade the guards outside her door and patrolling the garden, Eleanor would not have been left with her reputation in tatters, refusing to marry Haverford and unable to marry James.

If she had continued to refuse, had stayed true to her memories of him, and had not finally given way to her sisters' pleadings—for Lydia assured her that marriage would free her from the tyranny of her father and Helene had been set firmly on the shelf because of Eleanor's scandal—she would not have spent thirty-four years married to a monster. But her father and the Duke of Winshire told her James was dead, and after that it didn't matter what became of her?

They were mistaken, or they lied. Almost certainly, they lied. Now, James was back in England, and she would need to meet him and pretend that they hadn't broken one another's hearts so many years ago.

A few tears fell onto the letter, and then the Duchess of Haverford packed everything away, dried her eyes and returned the box to its place.

Weeping over the past and fretting over the future never helped.

She had children who loved her, friends, important work in her charities, and a full and busy life.

She smiled at her reflection in the mirror. Her complexion had returned to normal, and her sense of herself, too. The girl who mourned James had become a woman she rather liked. How could she regret any part of the path that led here?

2

Haverford House, London, April 1812

Eleanor had seen James—the Earl of Sutton, she supposed she must call him. Not that she would have a chance to call him anything. The Duke of Haverford had ordered his household and his dependents and allies to cut the entire Winshire family, and to refuse to attend entertainments where they were present.

Eleanor would have to make do with the glimpse last night at the Farningham ball. She had looked up when the room fell silent, and there he stood on the stairs, surrounded by members of his family, whom she barely noticed. James looked wonderful. More than thirty years had passed, and no person on earth would call him a fribble or useless now. He had been a king somewhere in Central Asia, and wore his authority like an invisible garment. And he was still as handsome as he had been in his twenties.

Eleanor caught herself sighing over James like a silly gosling. Silly, because women did not age as well as men, as the whole world knew. She no longer had the slender waist of a maiden, her hair was beginning to grey, and her face showed the lines her mother swore she would avoid if she never smiled, laughed, frowned, or showed any other emotion. Of course, she had not followed her mother's instruction, but those who had were no less lined than Eleanor, as far as she could see.

Besides, she was a married woman, and he was a virtuous man who had, by all accounts, deeply loved his wife. Even if he was willing and she was a widow, she would never take a lover. Somewhere within her might lurk the monster that was consuming her husband. Perhaps not. According to the physician, she had a better than even chance. But she would not know until she was sick, or until she was on her deathbed and still clean of the dreadful thing.

کمبل همه چیز برای عشق

Haverford Castle, East Kent, 1784
The Duke of Haverford did not bother with greetings or enquiries about Eleanor's health. He flung open the door without knocking and marched into Eleanor's sitting room, saying, "What is it, duchess? I have a great deal to do today."

Inwardly, Eleanor quailed as he stood over her, threat in every line of his posture. Unlike her father, he had never beaten her in cold blood, but she had every reason to fear his temper.

But fear would not serve her here. She was fighting for her life and for the wellbeing of her son. She maintained an outward semblance of calm and gestured to a chair. "Will you not be seated, Your Grace? As I said in my note, I have an important matter to discuss with you."

Haverford grumbled, but sat; even accepted a cup of tea. The delicate porcelain cup might not survive the next few minutes, but its sacrifice was a small price to pay for giving the discussion a façade of normality.

As she'd hoped, the good manners drilled into every English gentleman in the presence of a lady, even his wife, kept the duke sitting during the ritual of preparing the cup, but he burst out as soon as he accepted it from his wife's hand. "Well, duchess?"

Eleanor prepared her own cup, glad to have a reason not to look at him as she spoke. "Your Grace, you will be aware that I have been very ill this past six weeks. It is, indeed, why I removed myself to Haverford Castle."

"Yes, yes. And I'm glad to see you much improved, madam. I have need of you in London." He condescended to provide an explanation. "The bill I am sponsoring—those idiots who will not listen are much easier to convince after you've given them one of your excellent meals, and invited their wives and daughters to your soirees. How soon can you be ready to travel?"

What an excellent opening. "I can pack tomorrow and leave for London the day after, Your Grace."

Haverford smiled. "Excellent, excellent." He put the cup down, shifting as if to stand.

"If I do not have a relapse," Eleanor added.

Haverford sank back into his chair, frowning.

Now to get to the meat of the matter. Eleanor grasped hold of her dwindling supply of courage with both hands. *This is about saving Aldridge.* The situation in the nursery was fit to ruin him. His attendants had always indulged his every whim, egged on by the duke, who considered himself to be the only person the infant marquis needed to obey. Eleanor's frequent visits and threats of dismissal allowed him to be raised with some sense of structure and decorum. He knew she would not tolerate rudeness or temper, to her or to his nurses and the maids.

After spending four weeks too sick to leave her bed, she found the nursery in disarray, the young heir ruling the roost. He was in a wild tantrum when she arrived, and the next hour left her drooping with fatigue, and she still had to hunt down the boy's missing head nurse and find out why she had allowed such chaos to reign."

The memory prompted her to deal with the minor issue first. "Your affair with Aldridge's nurse, Your Grace."

He straightened, and opened his mouth, but Eleanor spoke over the rebuke that was certain to come. "I have no objection, sir, but I assume you have not given her license to neglect your heir or to be impertinent to me."

The duke frowned. "Certainly not. I shall have a word with the bitch."

"Thank you, Your Grace. You have always required others to treat me with the respect due to your wife, and that is why I was certain I could depend on you for what I am about to ask." Honey worked better than vinegar, one of the Haverford great aunts was fond of saying.

The duke smirked at the compliment and inclined his head, graciously indicating that she should continue.

Now for it. Best to say it straight out, as she had rehearsed a dozen times since she and Haverford's base-born half-brother, who was also his steward, had concocted the strategy. "You may be aware, Your Grace, that I have been taking the mercury treatment for the pox. As I am a faithful wife, and have only ever had intimate knowledge of one man—yourself, Your Grace—I must assume it originated with you."

As expected, Haverford erupted. "I will not—"

Eleanor held up a hand. "Your Grace has needs, and I would not normally comment on how you meet them, as long as any lovers you take within the household you have given me to manage are willing partners."

She kept talking over his attempt to interrupt, hoping his temper would not override his manners. "I owe you a second son, Your Grace, and I fully intend to attempt to carry out that side of our bargain, but I have a request to make to keep me safe from falling ill again."

He frowned, silenced for the moment. Eleanor thought it best to wait for him to speak. At least he was listening.

"Go on," he said at last.

"My doctor has assured me that fewer than half of all people who contracted second stage syphilis moved into the deadlier third stage, and most of those had the disease multiple times. Repeated infections may also kill or deform any further children we have. I would like to take steps to limit the risk, Your Grace."

"What steps?"

In the end, Haverford lost his temper twice more before he signed the document she put before him. In it, he promised to not to require intimacy from Eleanor unless he had refrained from any potential source of the disease for six weeks, and had been inspected by a doctor.

She had delicately hinted at the retribution that would follow if he didn't keep his word. A gentleman's word was his bond, of course, but only when given to other gentlemen. Haverford would not hesitate to break an agreement with his wife, if it suited him.

Thanks to the duke's training in politics, she knew all about the pressure to apply—in this case, the social contacts who would be informed of the whole disgusting situation if he broke his word. She had been a lady of the chamber to the Queen, was friends with several of the princesses, was sister to the current Earl of Farnmouth and sister-in-law to another earl and an earl's second son.

Added to that there were all of her social contacts. Those she had been presented with were only the start. Being Haverford's hostess had given her huge reach into the upper echelons of Society, especially those families headed by his political cronies and rivals.

One son, she contracted for, and a maximum of two more pregnancies. Eleanor prayed she would conceive quickly, that she would suffer no more miscarriages, and that she would deliver a healthy son without any further ado.

کمبل همه چیز برای عشق

Haverford House, London, April 1812

To give Haverford credit, Eleanor conceded, he had stuck to the agreement for several years. Her copy of the agreement was still in her secret compartment, somewhere. Her co-conspirator, Tolly Fitz-Grenford, had a second copy, and the third had been given to her brother in a sealed envelope, to be opened only if she died unexpectedly or sent a message asking him to read it.

Presumably, that copy was somewhere in the papers inherited by her nephew. Perhaps she should ask for it back, for Haverford had not approached her with marital duties in mind since she announced that she was *enceinte* with the child who proved to be the wanted spare son.

She very much doubted that he ever would. After all, his

mistresses and lovers were all twenty or thirty years younger than Eleanor.

On the other hand, he was behaving like a bad-tempered guard dog over James Winderfield's return, and she wouldn't put it past him to—mark his territory, as it were. The copies of the agreement had better stay where they were.

In truth, as long as the disease never recurred, Haverford had done her a favour. Without the incentive, she might have taken much longer to grasp what freedom she could.

Eleanor felt dizzy again, just thinking about James as he appeared last night. Haverford's command was not to be borne. Grace and Georgie were her dearest friends, and she was not going to be separated from them.

She would need to be careful, though. Perhaps one of her goddaughters could pass a note to one of Grace's daughters. The Society for the Betterment of Indigent Mothers and Orphans was meeting tomorrow. That would do nicely.

She moved to her escritoire, took out a sheet of her monogramed paper, and sharpened a quill. Now. Where could they meet? Perhaps Grace or Georgie might have a notion.

3

A *Haverford townhouse in Brighton, May 1812*
The package was stamped with the welcome postmark—
ST PETERSBORGH, all in capitals. Eleanor guessed its origins
when the butler brought it into the room, properly presented on a
salver. The package itself was anonymous from across the room, but
her butler's face, usually professionally impassive, told the tale. Only
dear Jonathan brought that lift to the corners of Parswarden's lips,
as if he was fighting a doting smile.

Sure enough, she recognised the slanting hand, just far enough
away from a scrawl to escape his tutor's heavy hand. She reached
out for it, grinning at Parswarden. "News from Jonathan," she
affirmed. "Wait while I open it, Parswarden, and I will give you
news to take below stairs."

Parswarden's smile almost escaped his control. "If Your Grace
would be so good, I am sure Cook would be pleased to hear how
our young lord is managing in those foreign parts. I will send for a
tea tray for Your Grace, while you open your package, shall I?"

Fifteen minutes later, the butler sailed out of the room, as close
to hurrying as his dignity would allow, eager to regale the upper

servants with stories of their young lord and his adventures: racing a troika—a sleigh pulled by three horses; dancing with a Russian imperial highness; hunting wolves with a wild band of Cossacks.

Eleanor shivered at the risks he took, but she had to admit that Jonathan led a charmed life, and waltzed through danger that made her hair curl. Indeed, he had been both charmed and charming since his birth.

She smiled as she sipped her tea. He had arrived after a further miscarriage, when she had almost lost hope that the birth of a son would deliver her from the consequences of her husband's lifestyle. Haverford had kept his word. As soon as it was certain that she was with child, he stopped visiting her, and before long she and her husband had established a pattern of separate lives, intersecting only when Eleanor would be a social or political asset to the duke.

Later that summer Haverford demanded she serve in such a role when he insisted on her joining him for a house party in Wales, where he wanted her assistance to impress a former ally who had changed sides. Later, she looked back on that chance meeting with the daughter of a local mine owner as a watershed moment in her life. The woman's son had the Haverford hazel eyes.

He arrived at her house a few months later, escaping his cruel grandfather after his mother's birth. In helping him, Eleanor discovered what became her life's passion: helping the helpless, particularly those with a call on His Grace or the Haverford family.

Perhaps it was not the life she had dreamed of, but she had made a difference in many lives. She mattered. Her pregnancy ended in a difficult birth, and it took her time to recover, but by the time Lord George Jonathan Creydon Walter Grenford received his unwieldy list of names at his baptism, the boy from Wales was established in her house. In her hidden cupboard, tied into a neat package, lay the notes that confirmed her in her path.

Haverford House, London, August 1787

Thomas Oliver, or Uncle Tolly as her son called him, balanced the delicate porcelain cup carefully on his knee, not taking his eyes off his hostess. A slow blink was his only reaction to her announcement that she intended to defy both Society and her husband. The Duke of Haverford was not a gentle man, and did not tolerate rebellion in his household. As his base-born brother, Tolly Fitz-Grenford had reason to know this fact at first-hand.

"The duke will not be pleased," he warned.

"His Grace will not wish to upset me." The duchess smiled serenely, and placed a hand on her middle. Tolly nodded his understanding. Eleanor had lost several babies since the son who secured the succession. Even His Grace would hesitate to counter his duchess's express commands when she might carry the backup hope of the Haverfords.

"Does His Grace know the boy is here?" Tolly asked.

"His Grace left London immediately after Jonathan's christening, Tolly, which gives me time. I would like to be armed with some information before he discovers David's presence.

"So, what, precisely, do you wish me to do?" Tolly asked.

Eleanor had her answer ready. "Talk to the boy, then trace back his steps and talk to the people he met on the way. I have made my own judgement based on my meeting with him and his mother. Your report will confirm or disprove that he is fit company for the Marquis of Aldridge and the baby. I believe him, Tolly, but I do not trust myself in such an important matter." She waved an impatient hand. "You understand. You are His Grace's half-brother, as David is half-brother to my sons."

Fitz-Grenford smiled, despite the caution he felt impelled to offer. "Unacknowledged half-brother, and the duke will bar the door to me if I presume on the relationship in the least. Very well, Your Grace. I shall see what I can find out."

کمبل همه چیز برای عشق

"Your Grace, enclosed please find reports of the interviews I conducted on your behalf into the journey of the boy David. He seems a nice lad. I will look forward to hearing how he goes on. Sincerely yours, Tolly.

کمبل همه چیز برای عشق

Gerald Ficklestone-Smythe
Manager of Cowbridge Mine, Llanfair

The boy was gone when I got back from the funeral. Little bastard. I told him I'd kick him to next Tuesday if dinner wasn't on the table, but nothing was prepared, and he was nowhere to be found. And he'd let the fire go out. He'll come back when he's hungry, and I'll have the skin off his back, see if I don't.

Where else is he going to go? London? To the duchess? My slut of a daughter, told the boy to go to the duchess when she was dead, but he is stupid if he thinks she's going to want her husband's by-blow, and so I told him when I took the money she'd left with his mother. I had a right to it, didn't I? I took his mother back after the duke had finished with her. I gave her a home. I even let her keep the boy.

The duke owed me that money. Yes, and more. Made a harlot out of my daughter, and turned her off with a measly few hundred pounds. Wouldn't pay more when that ran out. Then, when my daughter lay dying and couldn't keep house for me anymore, that pernicious swine sent his wife to steal the boy I raised, promising him I don't know what.

Now the bitch is dead, and the boy can't be found, but where could he have gone? He has no money for the coach fare, and it's a long walk to London, especially with winter coming on, and the Black Mountains between here and England.

He's no fool, the boy. He'll be back.

کمبل همه جیز برای عشق

Jeremiah Penchsnith
Captain of the Merry Molly, Bristol

We didn't find the lad till we was near Avonmouth. 'E was hid in the coal, but we saw 'im when 'e tried to escape over the side. 'E fair wriggled when we caught 'im, begged us to let 'im go. But 'e owed us 'is passage, and so I told him.

If we let away every lad who wanted a free trip over the Bristol Channel, we might as well set up as a ferry, and that's what I said.

Give the lad credit, 'e worked 'ard. Four trips 'e did wiv us, not counting the first. And then he left us in Bristol. I'd've kept 'im on, I would. Good worker, that lad. I 'ope 'e gets where 'e's going."

کمبل همه چیز برای عشق

Maggie Wakefield
Farmer's wife, Ditchford Frary, East Cotswolds

He was a mystery, young David. Turned up in a snow storm, he did. Bessie the dog found him when Matthew went out after the sheep, huddled up in the midst of the flock where they'd taken shelter in the lee of the old stone wall.

Matthew brought them all home: boy and sheep, the boy limping along on a stick because his ankle was swollen to twice its size. "I've a lamb for you to warm by the fire, mother," Matthew said, and then stood aside. Just a sprain, it turned out to be, but a bad one. I would not turn man or beast out in weather like that, let alone a boy, and no more would Matthew, so of course we let David stay.

Where did he come from in that awful weather? Wales, he said, but that couldn't be, could it? Wales is a long way away, across the wolds and then the water. And mountains, too, they say.

David was a good boy, so perhaps he was telling the truth. He made himself useful until he could walk again. He was a good hand in the kitchen, and he read to me and Matthew at night, which was a great blessing, for our eyes are not what they were. Not that I've ever read more than enough to piece together a few verses from the Bible. Not like David. It was a treat to listen to him, and I was sorry when he left.

But he had people waiting for him, he said, so off he went, off to London. We got him a lift as far as Oxford with Jem Carter. I hope he made it to his people. A fine boy like that? They would have been missing him, I'm sure.

کمبل همه چیز برای عشق

Sir Philip Westmacott
  Gentleman, London

My tiger? He's taken off. Ungrateful brat. Good boy with the horses, too. But there you go. That's what I get for taking a boy off the streets. I found him in Oxford, you know. Oh yes, I told you before, didn't I. He made sure I got back to my inn after a rather exciting evening. Didn't rob me, either, though he could have. I was somewhat—er—elevated.

I told him to come back in the morning for his reward, and he was waiting outside in the stable yard when I woke. And all he wanted was to come to London with me. I bought him a suit of clothing, of course. Couldn't be seen with him in the rags he had. Not livery. Not in Oxford. But I thought silver blue, to set off his dark hair. It would have looked stunning against my matched blacks.

We arrived late at night, and in the morning he was gone. Ungrateful brat.

کمبل همه چیز برای عشق

Henry Bartlett
  Gatekeeper, Haverford House, London

Of course I didn't let him in. A boy like that? Tidily dressed enough, and nicely spoken, but what child of substance is allowed to walk around the streets? But he wasn't a street urchin, neither. He asked if he could send a note, and he wrote it right there on a piece of paper I found him. Never was a street urchin that could read and write.

Anyway, I sent it in to the duchess. Told him he'd have to wait, but it wasn't but an hour before Her Grace's own maid came down to fetch him, and the next thing I knew, he was part of the household.

He seems a pleasant enough lad; always polite. But it just doesn't seem right, raising the duke's bastard under the same roof as his legal sons. The duke agrees, or so goes the talk in the servant's hall. But the duchess got her way, this time. And we're all to treat the boy as if he were gentleman. Her Grace has hired him a tutor, and word is he's off to Eton in the autumn. And the little Marquis follows him around like a puppy dog.

What will be the end of it, do you suppose?

کمبل همه چیز برای عشق

A Haverford townhouse in Brighton, May 1812

Eleanor opened the secret compartment of the escritoire that travelled everywhere with her. She didn't bother with Tolly's notes, but she did bring out the box of wooden toys that David had carved for his half-brothers. Aldridge's soldiers were particularly fine, the paint barely flaking. David had made them for Aldridge's twelfth birthday, and Aldridge never touched them again after Haverford threw David out.

Four-year-old Jonathan had been grief-stricken, though not as broken-hearted as Aldridge. Not that Aldridge spoke of it, then or later, but she'd seen the change in him; seen, too, the devastation he'd suffered when he and David met again, just a few years ago, only to be split even more decisively. That time, he'd admitted to Eleanor that he blamed himself: for Haverford's actions when he was twelve and David seventeen, and for the mistake that nearly cost David the life of the women he and Aldridge both loved.

Eleanor ran her hands over the scarred and dented head of the push-along toy David had made Jonathan so he wouldn't feel left out when Aldridge got his present. The stick to push it had long since gone. It had been Jonathan's favourite toy for years, till the pegs that made the legs move broke so they dangled, and the paint was completely worn away. A few specks of the bright colours it had been painted remained in the cracks. Eleanor kept it as a memento of the happy times with all three boys, when they stayed at Haverford Castle, and the duke did not.

Perhaps it could be repaired? If Jonathan ever married and had a son, she would like him to have it.

She chuckled at her own hopeful dreams. Certainly, nothing in

his letter indicated the approach of that day! And, to be fair, he had
no need to wed. He was a second son, independently wealthy, and
could please himself. She just wished he would do it in England.

4

Haverford House, London, June 1812

Eleanor had withdrawn to her private sitting room, driven there by His Grace's shouting. Her son, the Marquis of Aldridge, was as angry as she had ever seen him, his face white and rigid and his eyes blazing, but he kept his voice low; had even warned the duke about shouting.

"Let us not entertain the servants, Your Grace, with evidence of your villainy."

Unsurprisingly, the duke had taken exception to the cutting words and had shouted even louder.

Could it be true? Had Haverford paid an assassin to kill the sons of the man he insisted as seeing as his rival? An assassin with a pistol in the woods who had been caught before he could carry out his wicked commission.

His Grace's jealousy made no sense. Yes, James was back in England, but what did that matter to Haverford?

He had been furious when James and his family attended their first ball, and beside himself with rage when Society refused to accept that the prodigal returned was an imposter. She expected him to continue to attack the new Earl of Sutton with words. Even his petition to the House of Lords to have James's marriage declared invalid and his children base-born was typical of Haverford. But to pay for an assassin?

He had failed. She would hold onto that. And Aldridge was more than capable of holding his own.

As she sat there with her tea tray, sheltering from the anger of her menfolk, she gave thanks that her son had not been ruined by his father's dictates over how he should be raised. She had been able to mitigate some of the damage, but more than that, his younger brother Jonathan and his older half-brother David had been his salvation, giving him the confidence that he was loved and the awareness that he was not the centre of the entire world.

Aldridge's fundamentally loving nature helped, too. He was a rake, but not in his father's mould. Rather, he loved and respected women, even if he did treat them according to the stupid conventions applied to aristocratic males. And he was a good son.

Putting down her tea, she fetched a little box of keepsakes from her hidden cupboard. The fan her long dead brother had given her before her first ball. A small bundle of musical scores, that recalled pleasant evenings in her all too brief Season. Aldridge's cloth rabbit. She had retrieved it when Haverford had ordered it destroyed, saying his son was a future duke and should not be coddled. Aldridge had been eight months' old. Anthony George Bartholomew Philip Grenford, his full name was, but he had been born heir to his father, and therefore Marquis of Aldridge, and by Haverford's decree no one, not even Eleanor, called him by anything but his title.

Even so, the cloth rabbit had not been the first time she secretly defied her husband. She had been sneaking up to the nursery since Aldridge was born, despite the duke's proclamation that ladies of her rank had their babies presented to them once a day, washed, sweetly smelling and well behaved, and handing the infants back to their attendants if any of those conditions failed or after thirty minutes, whichever came first.

It was not enough for Eleanor, if she had grown bolder and

bolder and slowly taken control of her life, it was for their sweet sake.

کمبل همه چیز برای عشق

Hollystone Hall, December 1791

Eleanor poured tea for Tolly Fitz-Grenford, wondering if he would agree to her plan. After Haverford had exiled David and sent Aldridge off to school, she had pleaded with him to bring them both home, but he had laughed at her; pointed out that she had no power over him. In fact, he declared, her open defiance was enough to cancel the agreement they had made before Jonathan's birth.

So, she had then packed her bags and retreated to this lesser estate, the one place in the vast Haverford holdings that belonged to Her Grace and not His Grace.

"There, Tolly. Milk and no sugar. Is that not correct?"

Tolly took the cup. "Yes, Your Grace. Thank you."

She smiled. "We are brother and sister, Tolly. Will you call me 'Eleanor'?"

Tolly's face heated. As Eleanor knew, his relationship to the duke was not precisely a secret, but he had never been acknowledged. The father they shared had brought the son of a favourite mistress to be raised on the estate, and had even kept on his half-brother's tutor to train Tolly in the skills he would need to serve the duchy. Still, he had not been encouraged to show any familiarity, and the duke liked Tolly no more than Tolly liked the duke. "His Grace…"

Eleanor scowled. "I do not mean to concern myself ever again with the opinions of His Grace, except as I must for my safety and that of my children and the servants. Will you not call me by my name, Tolly, when we are not in company? Will you be my friend? For I stand in great need of one."

Tolly leaned forward to pat her hand. "I will always stand your friend, Eleanor," he told her.

"Good, for I need your help. Can you find me information with which to blackmail Haverford?"

Tolly blinked. Clearly, that was not what he expected.

"Blackmail?" he stuttered in response. "Is he… Has he…".

Eleanor pursed her lips, considering how much to tell him, then nodded decisively. "I shall be frank, Tolly. You shall not be shocked, for you know the duke even better than I do, in some ways. Some time ago, when he gave me a loathsome disease he picked up from one of his intimate companions, you helped me broker an agreement with him. He intends to repudiate the agreement. I intend to prevent him from doing so."

Tolly was reduced to stammering again. "I am sorry, Eleanor."

Eleanor waved off his commiserations. "I need to a truce with him, Tolly, for he has the power to keep my children from me. I wish to live apart, but in the same house. Will you find me the ammunition to bend him to my will?"

Tolly sat back. She knew he admired her. Would he be willing to fight the duke for her? It would not be easy. The Duke of Haverford was one of the most powerful men in the country. He feared little and was embarrassed by nothing.

She was relieved when he said, "I think I may be able to help, Eleanor. I have a couple of ideas."

Eleanor's smile broadened. "I have in mind to be a proper mother to my children; one who spends time with them as real mothers do, and also to do good for others with my position and my wealth. I can build a good life, Tolly, if I can just keep Haverford at arms' length."

Tolly narrowed his eyes as he thought. "I shall investigate, Eleanor. He will have secrets that will embarrass even him. I will find them for you."

"Thank you, Tolly."

He gave her a distracted smile as he continued to list strategies. "Entertainments," he said. "Eleanor, build alliances with the other great ladies of the ton and become a formidable hostess. You have it in you. If you have the support of the ladies, Haverford will have to think twice about acting against you."

Perfect! She knew he would be the right person to talk to. "And if I continue to host his political cronies and support his public life, he will have far less objection to my removing myself from his private one."

"You will have to fight him for influence over Aldridge," Tolly warned.

"I know," Eleanor agreed. "But I have an advantage there, my friend. I have never bullied or beaten my son." She lifted her cup as if it was filled with port or brandy rather than tea. "To my freedom, Tolly."

He grinned and returned the salute. "To your freedom."

کمبل همه چیز برای عشق

Haverford House, London, July 1812

She *had* been free, too; as much as a woman could be when married to the Duke of Haverford. She had been cautious about using the information that Tolly brought her. Haverford in a rage would ignore his own best interests, and any scandal would hurt her children and her other protegees as well as him. But usually, she had been able to live as she pleased.

She had considerable freedom, the opportunity to help others, and her children—what more could any woman expect?

At the firm rap on her door, she tucked the cloth rabbit away, slid the hidden compartment back into place and moved the panels to return the escritoire to its normal appearance. She knew that knock. "Enter," she called.

As expected, the visitor was Aldridge. Also as expected. He had been coming to her to be calmed after he'd worked himself into a fury since he was a little boy.

"Brandy, rather than tea, I think, my dear," she said to him. She was so proud of her son. In the silent battle for Aldridge's spirit, Haverford had done some damage, but the young marquis still retained his kindness and his innate decency. Eleanor was grateful for that.

5

Haverford House, London, July 1812

The Duchess of Haverford took tea in her rooms this quiet Monday afternoon. She was alone for once; even the maid who brought the tray sent off back to the servants' hall. Her life was such a bustle, and for the most part, that was how she liked it, but just for once, it was nice to have an afternoon to herself. No meetings. No entertainments to attend or offer. Not even any family members—her current companion had gone to visit her mother for her afternoon off, Aldridge was about his own business, her youngest ward was at lessons, and the two older girls had been invited on an outing with a friend.

As to Haverford, who knew where he was? But he would not disturb her here.

The thought had barely crossed her mind when a knock sounded; not the discreet tap of a servant, but a firm rap. *Not the duke. He wouldn't knock.* "Enter," she called.

Aldridge let himself into the room. He greeted her with his usual aplomb, asked after her day, but she could tell immediately that he was agitated. "What is wrong, my son?"

"I have no easy way to say this, Mama." He knelt before her and took her hands. "Sutton has been assaulted in the street, and his schoolroom party was also attacked. A runaway brewer's dray that was not a runaway at all." He squeezed her hands, pulling her back from her sudden dizziness. "Sutton gave his assailants a drubbing, and the children and their attendants are unhurt, thanks to swift action on the part of their escort."

Eleanor let out the air she was holding. "Thank goodness! And thank you, my dear, for letting me know before gossip made it so much worse."

Aldridge frowned slightly. "There is more. I heard of the assault on Sutton before it happened, and arrived with help just after. Mama, my secretary was asked to be the paymaster for the assailants. And guess who gave him the command."

She knew before her son said it. Breathed the words with him. "His Grace? Surely not. After the assassin at the duel, why would he do something like this again?"

"His Grace." Aldridge confirmed. He leapt to his feet and paced the room, not able to keep still for a moment, his body expressing the agitation his face refused to display. "He is getting worse, Mama. Whether it would have happened anyway, or whether the arrival of Sutton lit the flame, he lives on the point of explosion."

"I know, my dear." She knew better than Aldridge, in fact. Despite the long estrangement between her and her husband, they nonetheless lived in the same house, attended some of the same social gatherings, worked side-by-side for the same political causes. Aldridge kept largely to his own wing when he was under the same roof as his parents, which was increasingly rare. He managed all the vast business of the duchy, but Haverford had long since let go those reins to the extent that his only association with Aldridge tended to be through the bills and notes of hand that arrived regularly to be paid.

Aldridge thumped the mantlepiece. "This latest start... if word gets out that Haverford was behind the attack on Sutton and his family, it will be a disaster. Sutton would be well within his rights to demand Haverford's trial for attempted murder. This family is no stranger to scandal, Mama, and there's no doubt in my mind His Grace deserves to be hanged, silken noose or not, but…"

Eleanor's distress was such she found herself chewing her lip. "Thank God no one was seriously hurt."

"Thank Sutton and his sons for their warrior-craft, and my secretary for telling me in time to lead a rescue." Aldridge heaved a deep sigh and took another fast turn around the carpet. "He intended murder, Mama, and when I confronted him with it, he laughed and said he did it for England. He has gone too far, Mama. If he is found out, he puts us all at risk. What if the Regent decides to regard a murder attempt on another peer as treason?"

Eleanor had not considered that possibility. The title could be attained, the lineage considered corrupt. Aldridge had worked for years to rebuild the wealth of the duchy after his father's misman-agement. He could lose it all, including the title, and the Prince would be delighted to benefit.

Haverford had become more and more erratic as the year progressed. He insulted and alarmed other people at every event he attended, completely ignoring social conventions and saying what-ever he thought, often using the foulest of language. Thankfully, he was showing less and less inclination to go into Polite Society. Even so, the duchess frequently needed to use all her considerable tact and diplomacy to soothe ruffled feathers and quiet the gossip that claimed the duke was going mad.

"He is going mad," she acknowledged to her son, the one person in the world who could be trusted with the knowledge. "It is the French Disease, I am sure. It is rotting his brain."

"We cannot bring in doctors to examine him, Mama. Who knows what would come of that; what he would say and who they would tell? He cannot be allowed to continue, however."

Eleanor frowned. It was a conundrum. Who could prevent a duke from doing whatever he pleased?

Aldridge, apparently. "I have made arrangements. He has been persuaded to travel to Haverford Castle. When he arrives, trusted servants know to keep him there. He will be comfortable, Mama. I have arranged for him to be entertained, and have nurses on hand in case he needs them. The disease will kill him in the next year or two, probably, and he is likely to be bedridden long before the end."

He was brave, her son. He was breaking the laws of God and man in showing such disobedience to his father and a peer of the realm. She was sure God would understand, but the Courts might not. She would not ask about the entertainment Aldridge had provided. Knowing Haverford as she did, she did not want to know details. "He must never be set free," she concluded. Should anyone find out he was insane, the scandal would be enormous. Worse still for Aldridge.

"I understand that such spells may come and go, so we need to be prepared for him to return to sanity, at least for a time," Aldridge cautioned. "But if that does not happen, my instructions are to keep him from understanding he is imprisoned for as long as possible. With luck, the confusion in his mind will prevent him from ever working it out. I needed you to know, Mama, for two reasons. First, we need a story for the *ton*. Second, if he does not recover and if anything happens to me, it will be for you to keep him confined until Jon returns to be heir in my place."

"I hope dear Jonathan comes home soon, Aldridge. I miss my son. But do not speak of your demise, my dear. I could not bear it."

Aldridge stopped beside her and bent to kiss her forehead. "You are the strongest woman I know, dearest. Fret not. I am careful, and I intend to live to grow old."

Eleanor hoped so. She certainly hoped so.

After he left, she sat and stared at her escritoire, the concealer of her secrets. If Haverford's madness came out, what would it do her darling wards, the daughters of her heart? Her two eldest had only just made their debut this year, and the rumours about their origins made their lives hard enough!

Haverford House, London, May 1792

Tolly advised against the meeting. He said he would deal with Miss Kelly's problem. "I quite agree Haverford ought to do something to assist the opera dancer, given he is the immediate cause of the young female losing her job and needing to spend all her savings." Haverford would not, so it was for Tolly and Eleanor to intervene, as they had before. "You should not speak to such persons yourself," Tolly insisted. Tolly was quite firm on the subject, which Eleanor found sad, since his mother had been another such person.

Eleanor had insisted, so here was Miss Kelly, sitting in one of the smaller parlours at Haverford House, a delicate tea cup cradled in both hands.

She was exceptionally pretty; slender, with a heart-shaped face framed by dark curly hair, and blue eyes that were currently wide with wonder as she looked around the parlour.

The duchess allowed her a few minutes, until she overcame her curiosity and remembered her manners. "I beg yer pardon, Your Grace. It's rude, it is, to be staring at yer things like this. I can't be telling ye how grateful I am that ye agreed to see me."

"I must also admit to curiosity, Miss Kelly," Eleanor replied. "The gentleman who brought you here advised against my seeing you, but I ignored him."

The question, 'and why was that?' sparked in Miss Kelly's expressive eyes, but she simply repeated, "I am grateful."

Eleanor leaned forward to examine the unfortunate consequence of Miss Kelly's association with the Duke of Haverford, currently asleep in a basket at Miss Kelly's feet. The little girl was well wrapped against the cold, but the tiny face was adorable. Dark wisps of curl had escaped from the knitted bonnet, and a tiny hand clutched the blanket, pink dimples at the base of each chubby finger.

"My friend tells me that you seek a home for the baby," Eleanor commented.

Miss Kelly heard the question. "I cannot be taking her home, you see. I have a chance… There's a man. He wanted to wed me when my Ma and Pa died, but I had my head full o' dreams. He went home without me, but he'll take me yet. He knows how it is for girls like me. He'll not blame me for not being a maid, but —
Patrick is a proud man, Your Grace. He'll not raise another man's babe. Or if he does, he'll make it no life for her, and we'd finish up hating one another and the poor wee girleen."

Eleanor could see the point. "So, you will leave her behind."

Miss Kelly must have assumed a criticism in that. "I'd keep her if I could, Your Grace, but here in London? How can a girl like me earn enough to support her and keep her with me? I want a good home for her; somewhere safe where she can grow up to better than her Ma. Then what happens to me don't matter, so I might as well take Patrick as not. Better than another protector. Leastwise, if I get another baby in my belly, I'll have a man to stand by me."

As Haverford had not. He had turned his pregnant mistress out of the house in which he'd installed her, with a few pounds to 'get rid of the brat'. Miss Kelly did not have to tell Eleanor that part of the story. She knew it well enough from past liaisons. Tolly proposed to find a childless couple who wanted a daughter to love.

At that moment, the baby opened her eyes, looked around with apparent interest, then fixed her gaze on Eleanor, or — more probably — on the diamonds sparkling in Eleanor's ear bobs. The little treasure smiled, and reached up her arms, babbling an incomprehensible phrase.

Eleanor was on her knees beside the basket, reaching for the dear child before she thought to look up and ask permission. "May I?"

When she called for her secretary, thirty minutes later, little Matilda was still in Eleanor's arms. "Ah. Clara. This is Miss Kelly. She will be staying in the nursery for the next few days. I need you to hire me a wet nurse and a nanny to look after Matilda after Miss Kelly leaves. I also want to purchase a smallholding in — Kinvara, was it not? It shall be your dowry, Miss Kelly."

It was nearly five months before the Duke of Haverford discovered that the nursery, recently vacated by his younger son Jonathan, was once again occupied. He was moved to challenge his wife on her presumption, but her only response was to tell him the child's full name — Matilda Angelica Kelly Grenford — and to add that the scandal of her presence was long past, but the scandal of her removal would be ongoing. As his duchess and a leading figure in Society, the woman had the power to make the outrageous threat stick. He dealt with the impertinence in his usual fashion. He left, and never mentioned the little girl's existence again.

كمبل همه چيز براى عشق

Haverford House, London, July 1812

She had intended only the one—a daughter to satisfy the longing for a little girl to raise and love. But fate had other ideas, and the second child arrived within a matter of months.

كمبل همه چيز براى عشق

Haverford House, London, September 1792

When Mrs Watterson had asked for this meeting, she had seemed so nervous that the Eleanor had offered to meet her in the housekeeper's sitting room, thinking the woman might be more at ease on her own ground. It had made no appreciable difference. The housekeeper sat bolt upright, not sipping from her cup, her knuckles white with tension, her voice strained as she tried to make conversation.

Mrs Watterson praised the baby, little Miss Matilda, reminding Eleanor that she would far rather be upstairs in the nursery than down here in the cluttered little room, where the furniture was over-stuffed and the fire too hot.

Eleanor was discovering the joys of mothering a baby, and would have spent the whole day in the nursery with her little ward, had her duties allowed. The duchess was a mother twice over, but both the ducal heir and the spare had been taken from her at birth, handed over to a retinue of servants, and thereafter presented for a ceremonious inspection for a few minutes a day whenever she and they happened to be in the same residence.

When Aldridge was born, she had been so oppressed by her marriage and the expectations that crushed her, she had accepted the duke's dictate: that aristocratic women had little to do with the children they produced for the well-being of the title. By the time Jonathan arrived, she had recovered some of her confidence, but the pregnancy and birth, coming after years of miscarriages, left her frail both emotionally and physically, and her little boy had been six months old when she wrested control of the nursery from the despot who had ruled there since Haverford appointed her in the early days of their marriage.

The woman had been gone for more than five years, and sweet little Matilda was in the care of her replacement: a woman chosen by Eleanor, with testimonials from people Eleanor trusted, and completely devoid of the physical attributes that were the only qualifications of interest to the duke when he interviewed a female for any position.

An apology dragged Eleanor's attention back to the conversation. Mrs Watterson had finally begun to approach the matter that had her so anxious. "Forgive my impertinence, Your Grace," she said, "but is it true that Miss Matilda... that her mother...?"

Seeing Eleanor's raised brows, she rushed on. "I don't ask out of idle curiosity, ma'am. It is just that..."

All suddenly became clear. Eleanor sighed. "One of the maids? Or a villager's child?"

Much of the tension rushed out of Mrs Watterson, expelled in a huff of air. "My niece, Your Grace. I would not have said anything, but..." Tears began to roll down the pale cheeks.

Eleanor patted her hand. "I shall help, of course. A pension. A place to live in a village where she isn't known."

Mrs Watterson shook her head, the tears increasing in volume. Eleanor suppressed a sigh for her lost afternoon with Matilda, and devoted her energies to soothing the housekeeper and eliciting the rest of the story.

It was a sad one, but one she had heard before during nearly fifteen years of marriage to the Duke of Haverford. Jessie, the orphaned daughter of Mrs Waterson's only sister, worked for a neighbouring household. "I would not have her in this house, Your Grace, saving your pardon," the housekeeper said. It did not save the girl. She was returning from an errand to the village when a gentleman (Mrs Watterson began 'His Gr...' then changed the word) overtook her on the road. He saw that she was young and pretty, and led her off into the woods on the side of the road. Having exercised what he regarded as his rights, he rode on his way.

Jessie told no one until six months later, when one of the maids with whom she shared a room noticed the swelling she had managed, until then, to conceal. Of course, she was dismissed, but her aunt found her lodgings in the village, and paid for her keep and the services of the midwife. "It was a hard birth, Your Grace," Mrs Watterson explained. "Little Jessica survived, but my niece did not. I'm the only kin she has, poor little baby, and what is to become of her?"

Haverford had only just noticed Matilda, and had not been pleased. Eleanor had managed to threaten him in a way that did not cause his unstable temper to explode. Another of his by-blows in his nursery might be a straw too far, and when Haverford was angry, he cared nothing for consequences.

On the other hand, Matilda would benefit from growing up with another little girl of much the same age. The seven-year age gap between Aldridge and Jonathan meant they both lacked companionship, except for that of their servants.

Eleanor temporised. "Where is the baby now, Mrs Watterson?"

"The midwife knew a woman who could feed her, Your Grace, having recently lost her own youngest. Mrs Fuller. It was the best I could do, ma'am, but I don't want to leave her there."

Eleanor didn't blame her. Cold, neglect, and disease carried off Mrs Fuller's children with alarming frequency. She was one of those women that every village seems to produce almost certainly not entitled to the honorific, making a living for herself and her surviving offspring by serving drinks and food in the local tavern, and other more intimate services wherever a man with a coin might care to take her. Eleanor had tried to help the female into an honourable job, but whether she was too beaten down by life or just preferred earning her living on her back, the experiment had not worked out.

Eleanor stood. "Very well, Mrs Watterson. We shall visit Mrs Fuller and meet little Jessica. Then we shall see."

She had, of course, already made up her mind. No need to tell His Grace this was another of his unwanted children. This time, she would not even wait until he noticed. She would simply announce that she had taken in another orphan to keep Matilda company. She would not discuss the child's origins. As long as he did not feel she was censuring his behaviour, he probably wouldn't care.

کمبل همه چیز برای عشق

Haverford House, London, August *1812*

Her strategy had worked very well, and she had gloried in her two little girls. Haverford's disinterest had the benefit that she did not need to counter his influence in choosing servants or selecting tutors. She had no need to fear he would suddenly command the children's attendance and carry them off to activities that no child should witness.

Indeed, the presence of their little sisters had much to do with the sweetness of character both of her sons managed to retain, and the truth that their treatment of women was so much better than their father had taught them.

Aldridge would get Haverford to the castle, and Eleanor must go and prepare for an evening in Society. The future of her girls might depend on the social alliances she strengthened tonight.

It was some time later that Eleanor realised Aldridge hadn't asked, and she hadn't explained, why she needed to hear that Sutton was unhurt before the rest of Society got hold of the story. Had anyone been listening, they would think that Sutton was more to her than a fond memory.

6

Haverford House, London, July 1812

As soon as she arrived home, Eleanor ordered a tea tray to her room and then sent the servants away. Her visit to Miss Clemens' Oxford Street Book Palace and Tea Rooms had left her trembling, but gloriously happy.

Grace and Georgie had been unable to attend their arranged meeting, but James had come in their stead. No, Sutton. No, James. She would call him James in her own thoughts. She had seen him, of course, in the street or at various entertainments. But to see him up close—to touch him, even with her gloved hands! To talk with him for upwards of half an hour, just the two of them, alone!

Ah, she was every kind of fool. The Earl of Sutton was famous for having defied his father to remain with the Persian princess he married; the mother of his children. They had spoken of her today, the Princess Mahzad. James loved her still; it was in every word he spoke of her. Poor James, a widower for more than a decade.

But they had talked! It was a gift beyond price. Perhaps, when all this nonsense with Haverford was over, she and James could be friends?

Haverford House, London, 1794

116

The two ladies having tea with Eleanor clearly had something on their minds. They kept exchanging glances, and frowning at the servants who bustled in and out. Eleanor was entertaining two dear friends on this lovely day in 1794; Lady Sutton, daughter-in-law to the Duke of Winshire, and Lady Georgiana Winderfield, his daughter.

As the servants wheeled in the refreshments Eleanor had ordered, and made sure that the ladies had everything they required, the three friends spoke of the fashions of the current season, the worrying events in France, the reopening of the Drury Theatre, and their children.

As the last of the servants left, Eleanor spoke to her companion-secretary, a poor relation of her husband whom she was enjoying more than she expected. Largely because she had decided to find the girl a match, and was gaining great entertainment from the exercise. Eleanor could hit two birds with a single stone if she sent dear Margaret to her husband's office, where his secretaries currently beavered away over the endless paperwork of the duchy. "Margaret, Lady Sutton and Lady Georgiana have a wish to be private with me. I trust you do not mind, my dear, if I send you on an errand? Would you please ask that nice Mr Hammond to find the accounts for Holystone Hall? I wish to go over the coal bills." Margaret blushed at the mention of Theseus Hammond, and left eagerly. Very good.

Grace was diverted. "Matchmaking, Eleanor?"

"A little. He is as poor as a church mouse, of course. We shall have to see if we can find a position in which he could support a wife. But what is it you wanted to tell me?"

Grace and Georgie exchanged glances, then Georgie leaned forward and took Eleanor's hand between two of hers. "We thought you should hear it from us, first. Word will undoubtedly be all over Town in no time."

Georgie's unexpected touch alarmed Eleanor. Embracing — even touching — was Not Done. A kiss in the air beside a perfumed cheek, but nothing more. Except for her son Jonathan, who was fond of cuddles, no one had held Eleanor's hand since Aldridge crept from the schoolroom to sit all night with her after her last miscarriage. "What can possibly be wrong? Not something Haverford has done?" But what could such a powerful duke do to give rise to the concern she saw in the eyes of her friends.

"Not Haverford." Georgie again exchanged glances with her sister-in-law. "His Grace our father received a letter of condolence on the death of my brother Edward." Another of those glances.

"Out with it, Georgie," Eleanor commanded. "I am not a frail ninny who faints at nothing. Tell me what you think I need to know."

Georgie sighed, and firmed her grip on Eleanor's hand. "Eleanor, the letter was from James."

Who was James? Not Georgie's brother, the one love of Eleanor's life. James was dead, killed by bandits nearly fifteen years ago. They got the letter. The Duke of Winshire himself told her. She was shaking her head, shifting herself backwards on the sofa away from Georgie, whose warm compassionate eyes were so much like those of her missing brother. Missing?

"Not dead?" Her voice came out in an embarrassing squeak, as emotions flooded her. Joy. Anger. A desperate sadness for so many years lost to grieving.

"Alive," Georgie said. "James is alive, Eleanor."

The room spun and turned grey, and Eleanor knew no more.

کمبل همه چیز برای عشق

Haverford House, London, July 1812

After that, from time to time, her friends had shared smuggled letters with her. Not often. A year or more might pass before another message made its way across the vast distance between James's mountain kingdom north of Persia and his sister in England. Often enough, though, that Eleanor shared in the delight of two more children, the grief of his wife's death, weddings for four of his children and the birth of grandchildren.

She hadn't told him that she knew much of what he told her today. Hearing the stories in his own dear voice was such a pleasure. She smiled again. Yes. Surely, one day they could be friends?

7

Haverford *House, London, October 1812*
Despite hundreds of servants, the house seemed quiet. Haverford was in Kent with his own attendants, though his condition appeared to be improving. Aldridge was touring the ducal estates, keeping a tight hand on the reins of the vast lands that underpinned the Haverford wealth.

She was used to their absence. But for once, she had no one else. Her current companion was off with friends, finishing the initial planning for this year's Christmas house party and New Year's Eve Ball, and the girls were visiting friends in the country.

She had seen James again, today. This time, it had been planned. She had sent him a note to tell him she would be at the bookshop, and giving the time her meeting ended. Afterwards, she had been sure he wouldn't come, and if he did, he would think she was chasing after him.

She pushed away the tea tray; she didn't want it. What she wanted was in the secret compartment; a memory she could not quite believe and could never forget. She found the little box, and extracted a crumbling faded rose. She had plucked it from her garden at Haverford Castle after a memorable dream, as a reminder that James had given his heart elsewhere.

Haverford Castle, near Margate, July 1795

Cecily was older. Of course, she was. More than fifteen years had passed since the season they shared; the season that ended with Eleanor's broken heart and Cecily's marriage. She and her husband Alec had taken a long wedding trip, to see the Orient, they said. And then… nothing. Until she appeared again in England, just a few weeks ago.

Through the ritual of greeting, of inviting her guest to be seated, of preparing a cup of tea for each of them, Eleanor kept shooting glances, comparing the composed and still lovely woman before her with the gangling clumsy teen Eleanor had taken under her wing at first meeting. She glowed with happiness, but the lines barely visible on her brow and around her eyes spoke of suffering and pain. What had happened in all those years away?

They spoke of nothings: the weather, the fashions, who was and who wasn't in Town, until all of the maids had left the room and they were alone. Then they both spoke at once.

"Did you wish to hear of…?" Cecily began.

"Lady Sutton and Lady Grace Winderfield tell me…" said Eleanor, stopping herself and waving her hand for Cecily to carry on.

Cecily nodded, as if Eleanor had confirmed what Cecily had been about to ask. "I met with Lord James Winderfield late last year. That is what you wished to know, is it not, Your Grace? Where I saw him, and how?"

"It is," Eleanor agreed, grateful that decades of training and practice allowed her to keep her face and posture from reflecting her inner turmoil. "His sisters told me he was alive, but little more." Married. To an Eastern princess. With children. Happy, or so Cecily had told them. It was silly to feel hurt. Did she expect him to wear the willow for her for a lifetime? She did for him, but look at the alternative! She had never been given the least incentive to fall in love with the tyrant she had been forced to marry. She was glad James was happy. Of course, she was. Or would be, given time.

Cecily had kept on talking while she scolded herself, asking her something. Ah. Yes. Was she certain she wished to know the details?

"You loved him, once," Cecily said, her voice kind.

She could answer that. "He was a dear friend, Mrs McInnes, and I have grieved him as dead these many years. I would dearly love to know how he survived, and how he now lives. And he has children, his sisters say. Many children. Please. Start at the beginning and tell me all about him."

That night, Eleanor had a very vivid dream.

She found herself in a beautiful garden. It was a long rectangle, walled on three sides and on the fourth bounded by steps up to a house. Or perhaps a castle, though unlike any castle Eleanor had ever seen. A fort of some kind, its arches and domes giving it an exotic air entirely in keeping with the garden.

A pool divided the garden in half; no, in quarters, for it had two straight branches stretching almost to the walls from the centre point of the walled enclosure. Eleanor had woken to find herself in one quadrant of the garden, surrounded by flowers in a myriad of colours, some familiar and some unknown. Not woken. She could not possibly be awake. Nowhere in England had the mountains she could see over the walls, and nor was this an English garden.

She must have spoken the last thought, because a voice behind her said, "Not English, no. Persian, originally, though I am told they are found from Morocco to Benghal. It is a *chahar bāgh*; a Paradise garden."

Eleanor turned. Behind her, a lady as exotic as her garden stood on the steps of a pavilion, raised to give a sheltered place from which to enjoy a view over the garden. "I am asleep and dreaming, I think," the lady said, "for it is afternoon by the sun, and at such a time my garden is full of my children and my ladies." She waved to indicate the deserted space, her lips gently curved and her face alight. "We should enjoy the peace while it lasts. Will you join me for coffee, or perhaps tea?"

Eleanor nodded and mounted the stairs to join her, following her into a space as alien as the garden, the stone-paved floor almost invisible under brightly coloured rugs and cushions. "Is it your dream or mine? For when I went to sleep, I was in Haverford House, in London. And this is not England."

The lady raised both brows, and then let them drop, her face suddenly bland. "You are, perhaps, the Duchess of Haverford?"

"Forgive me, I should have introduced myself. Yes, I am Eleanor Haverford."

If Eleanor had any doubts that this was a dream they were dispelled in the next instant, when a small table appeared from thin air, laden with a tea pot, a long full-bellied coffee pot, two cups, and plates of small delicacies.

The lady gave a brief huff of amusement. "The dream reminds me of my manners. Please be seated, duchess. Your Grace, is it not? I am Mahzad."

Now it was Eleanor's turn to wipe all expression from her face as she inclined her head. "Your majesty. Is that the correct form of address? Cecily McInnes spoke of you when she returned to England."

"Please call me Mahzad. After all, we have a lot in common, you and I. Tea? Or coffee?"

"Coffee, and please call me Eleanor. Cecily said he was well, and very much in love with his wife." And Eleanor was happy for the man she had once loved with a maiden's ardent passion. Of course, she was.

Mahzad smiled and placed a protective hand over her belly, where a slight rounding indicated yet another child on the way to join the already large family. "You have a generous heart, Eleanor. You have not been as fortunate as James and I; I think."

Eleanor waved away the sympathy. "I have my children and my work. I am content. But tell me about your family. Who knows how long the dream might last, and I wish to know all about them."

Haverford House, London, July 1812

It was her imagination, of course, building on the stories that Cecily had told, and Grace and Georgie before her. But the following morning, Eleanor had found a newly unfurled rose in the castle gardens that was the precise shade of the roses in one part of Mahzad's garden.

Now, it was fragile, dried and faded, adorned with yet another tear to join all the others she had wept on it in the past eighteen years. James had loved his wife, but he had loved her first. He had assured her that he had fully intended to come home and claim her, but that his father denied to pay his ransom, despite his captor's threat to execute him without it.

To add insult to injury, Winshire had told James that Eleanor was already married to Haverford. It was true, but only because Winshire and Eleanor's father had assured her that James was dead.

Eleanor gently laid the flower back into the box. Once, she had loved and been loved. That, at least, would never change.

8

H*averford Castle, East Kent, November 1812*
Eleanor was pleased to spend a few hours on her own. Haverford, having recovered his senses, was making up for lost time at some scandalous house party. Aldridge was in London, though he had not shared his reasons. Eleanor's wards had accompanied her to Kent, but they had gone to stay with friends for a few days, even Frances, who at nearly fifteen was old enough to begin venturing into polite company in the more relaxed environment of the country.

She smiled at the escritoire that travelled from home to home with her. Hidden in its depths were the first booties she had ever knitted. And reknitted, multiple times, until she got it right. Matilda had worn them, and then Jessica.

Frances, though, was already out of infancy when she joined the Haverford household. There was never any doubt Eleanor would keep her, of course. She could not deny Jonathan and Aldridge; and besides, she fell in love with the little girl at first sight.

Haverford Castle, East Kent July 1806

The Duchess of Haverford examined her two sons as they waited for her to pour them a cup of tea each. To an outsider, they would seem totally at ease — Aldridge relaxed on the sofa, an amused twist to his lips and his cynical eyes fond as he teased his brother about the horse the boy had bought on a jaunt into Somerset; Jon laughing as he defended his purchase, suggesting warmly that the marquis's eye for a filly blinded him to the virtues of a colt.

To their fond Mama, they appeared worried. Eleanor saw strain around the younger man's eyes, and quick darting glances at her and then at his brother when Jon thought she wasn't watching. Aldridge had that almost imperceptible air of being ready to leap to Jon's defence in an instant; a watchfulness, a vague tension.

Aldridge's cup was prepared as he liked it, and he came to fetch it from her hands, thanking her with a smile.

She would let them raise the subject, if that was their plan, but she did not intend to let them leave this room without knowing about the new addition to her nursery: a nervous withdrawn little girl of three or four years old. "If she was a bumptious little lordling and not a poor trembling mouse," Nanny said, "she could be one of my lads come again. Same shaped face and eyes. Same colour hair with the curls that won't brush out. Their lordships have your eyes, Your Grace, and this wee sprite doesn't, but I'll tell you who has eyes just that colour: so close to green as never so." Not that Nanny did tell the duchess. She did not need to. Those eyes were more familiar to Eleanor than her own.

She handed a cup to the younger son of the man with those eyes.

The child came from Somerset. Jon had brought her home in his curricle, leaving his groom to ride Jon's horse and manage the colt. On finding out about the little girl, and learning that Jon had deposited her in the nursery and then gone straight out to search town for his older brother, Eleanor had been tempted to question the groom.

However, she wanted Jon to tell her the story. Or Aldridge, perhaps. It was more likely to be his story than Jon's, given the age of the child. Jon was only 19. Furthermore, it was in Somerset that a certain outrageous scandal blew up five years ago, resulting in the exile of the sons of two dukes: Aldridge to a remote Haverford estate in northern Scotland, and his accomplice overseas.

Nanny didn't think the little girl was old enough to be a souvenir of Aldridge's visit to the Somerset town, but her size might be a result of neglect. She had been half-starved, poor little mite. The bruises might be from falls or other childhood accidents. Nanny suspected beatings, which made Eleanor feel ill to think about.

She sat back with her own cup, and took a sip. As if it were a signal, Jon gave Aldridge another of those darting glances and spoke.

"Mama, I expect you've heard about Frances."

Ah. Good. She was to be told the story. "Is that her name, Jon? Nanny didn't know it, and little Frances isn't talking."

Jon nodded, and smiled. There was a sweetness to the boy that the elder never had, perhaps because he was a ducal heir from the moment of his birth. "She is a little shy, Mama." His smile vanished and he frowned. "She has been badly used, and for no fault of her own. I could not leave her there, Mama. You must see that."

Eleanor arched one brow, amusement colouring her voice as she answered. "If you tell me her story, my son, we will find out."

It was much as Eleanor already suspected, though the villain in the piece was neither of her sons. Lord Jonathan Grenford, arriving in Fickleton Wells to inspect and pay for the offspring of a horse pairing that he coveted, found that the whole town, except for the owner of the horse, gave him a cold shoulder, and no one would tell him or his groom why.

Only on the last night of his stay did he hear the story. He came back to his hotel room to find a woman waiting for him. "A gentlewoman, Mama, but with a ring on her finger, and quite old — maybe 30. I thought... well, never mind that."

Aldridge gave a snort of laughter, either at Jon's perspective on the woman's age or at his assumption about her purpose.

Jon ignored him. "Anyway, I soon realised I was wrong, for there on the bed was a little girl, fast asleep. The woman said she belonged to Haverford, and I could take her. I argued, Mama, but I could see for myself she was one of us, and that was the problem. The woman's husband had accepted Frances when she was born, but as she grew, she looked more and more like her father."

"He resented being cuckolded, I suppose," Eleanor said, "Men do, my sons, and I trust you will remember it."

Both boys flushed, the younger one nodding, the older inclining his head in acknowledgement, the glitter in his eyes hinting he did not at all appreciate the gentle rebuke.

"He took his frustrations out on Mrs Meecham, which she surely didn't deserve after all this time when I daresay he has sins of his own, and on little Frances too, which was entirely unfair. Mrs Meecham said that if Frances remained as a reminder, the Meechams could never repair their marriage, and that she feared one day he would go too far and seriously hurt or even kill the baby. So, I brought her home. Can we keep her, Mama?"

Eleanor looked at Aldridge, considering.

"She is not mine, if that is what you are thinking, Mama," her eldest son told her. "She might have been, I must admit, but she was born fifteen months after I was last in Fickleton Wells. I'd been in Scotland for six months when Mrs Meecham strayed outside of her pastures again."

Six months after the scandal, His Grace the duke had travelled back to Somerset, to pay damages to the gentlemen of Fickleton Wells who claimed that their females had been debauched. He had greatly resented being made a message-boy, and had been angry with his son and the females he had shamed for their indiscretions and beyond furious at the cuckolded gentlemen of the town for imposing on his ducal magnificence with their indignation. The mystery of Frances's patrimony was solved.

"She is so sweet, Mama, and has been through so much. She needs tenderness and love. Don't tell me I must give her to foster parents or an orphan asylum. I know His Grace will not be pleased, but…"

Eleanor smiled. "The problem with Fickleton Wells, Jon, as I'm sure Aldridge is aware, is that it is a Royal estate. Wales was mightily annoyed at what he saw as an offence against his dignity. He insisted on Haverford making all right."

Jon's shoulders slumped. He clearly thought this presaged a refusal.

Aldridge was seven years more sophisticated and had been more devious from his cradle. His eyes lit again with that wicked glint of amusement. Eleanor nodded to him. "Yes, Aldridge, precisely."

Aldridge put down his cup. "Wales is not best pleased with His Grace at the moment. A matter of a loss at cards."

Eleanor and her elder son grinned at one another, and her younger son perked up, looking from one to the other.

"Should one be grieved by the loss of a fostering," Eleanor mused, "and take one's sorrows to, let us say, a Royal princess who might be depended on to scold her brother for the behaviour of one of his favourites…" Eleanor stopped at that. Jonathan did not need the entire picture painted for him. He gazed at her, his eyes wide with awe.

"His Grace will not dare make a fuss. If His Royal Highness finds out that the very man he sent to save him from the offended citizens left a cuckoo in the nest of an esteemed leader of the community…"

"Precisely," Aldridge agreed. "Mama, you are brilliant, as always."

The duchess stood, leaving her cup on the table, and both boys. "Let us, then, go up to the nursery, and make sure all is well with your new baby sister."

کمبل همه چیز برای عشق

Haverford Castle, Kent, November 1812

Haverford had not even hinted at coming to her rooms since Jonathan had brought Frances to join her nursery—the little girl a greater gift than her son could ever know. The scandal of the child's existence was a secret Haverford needed to keep from his royal cousins, and she had been able to use her knowledge of that secret to secure her wards' future under Haverford's reluctant and anonymous protection, and to ensure her continued freedom from his intimate attentions.

It had been an unpleasant negotiation, determined on her part and rancorous on his—not that he much wanted his aging wife, but he resented having his will forced. In return for his agreement, she had promised to continue as his political hostess, and to maintain the myth of a perfect Society marriage.

Why was she spoiling a perfectly good afternoon thinking about His Grace? She came up here to explore quite different memories.

9

____

ollystone Hall, December 1812
The Duchess of Haverford waved her dresser away and stood so she could better see Matilda, Jessica, and Frances. Yes, even Frances was to go to tonight's fancy-dress ball, for a short while and under the strict supervision and care of her sisters.

How lovely they were! Matilda and Jessica had faced a difficult first Season with grace and courage. Even Eleanor's influence could not overcome their murky origins. Society could be remarkable stupid.

Eleanor had had high hopes of the Earl of Hamner, although he also showed an interest in Lady Felicity Belvoir. If he did not stay the course, somewhere out there was a man who would look past Matilda's parentage to her beautiful nature: her kindness, her intelligence, all the wonderful qualities that made Eleanor so proud of her.

Jessica was more of a worry in a way, covering her hurt at any snubs by layering on more charm, until she skirted the edge of flirting. Perhaps there was someone here at this house party who could give Jessica the love she needed?

At least Frances was safe for a couple more years, and perhaps, by the time she made her debut, her sisters would be married and able to help her.

In some ways, Eleanor wished they were all still in the schoolroom.

Haverford Castle, July 1810

Eleanor paused in the doorway of the schoolroom, where her three foster daughters were drawing under the supervision of their governess. The subject was a collection of objects: a flower in a rounded glazed bowl, a trinket box open to display a set of coral beads that trailed over the edge onto the polished surface of the table, a delicate statuette of a gun dog, with proudly pointing muzzle.

A difficult composition for such young girls, though little Frances was talented, and the older two girls competent enough. At thirteen, Frances had inhabited the Haverford nursery floor for eleven years, and by the time of her debut, in three or four years, the scandal of her existence was likely to be minimal. Especially since she, least of the three, resembled their shared father.

Matilda would face the ton first. At sixteen, she was as much a beauty as her mother had been, with the dark hair and stunning figure that had made her mother a reigning beauty of the *demimonde*, though she was only an opera dancer. A brave one, too, who—given the chance to start a new life back in her homeland of Ireland— braved Haverford House to beg for a safe home for her daughter, perhaps a tenant farm on an out-of-the-way Haverford estate.

It was just chance that Haverford was away on that occasion, and that Eleanor had just been arriving home. Or an intercession of the divine. Haverford would have turned his full ducal rage on a scion of the local gentry, and denied everything. But Eleanor took the baby in her arms and fell in love.

She smiled as she watched the three heads bent in concentration. It had taken His Grace nine months to realise that his nurseries were once again occupied, and by then Jessica, some six months younger and the daughter of a pretty maid who once attracted Haverford's attention. The combination was lethal, for the girl had died in childbirth, and the grieving grandmother brought the baby to Haverford House, to Eleanor. No-one could doubt Jessica's parentage. She and Lord Jonathan, Eleanor's second son, were as alike as male and female could be.

Haverford, of course, denied that he'd sired the two girls, and ignored them completely. His solution to the unfortunate results of his careless whoring was to blame the female, a bag of coins (carefully measured to their social position) the only assistance they could expect.

Thank goodness she had been strong enough to hold out for the right to keep the children. As long as he never saw them, was not expected to acknowledge them in any way, and provided nothing extra for their support, he chose to treat her fostering as an eccentric hobby.

Frances had been the third, her birth a scandalous secret even Haverford did not want disclosed. Eleanor loved the three girls with all her heart, loved them as fiercely as she loved her two sons. And she could not regret bringing them into her home, selfish of her though it was.

She had learned better, especially after the disastrous end to David Wakefield's time under the Haverford roofs. For years now, she had been quietly settling her husband's by-blows in less scrutinised households, carefully supervised to ensure they had the love and care she wanted for those who shared blood with her sons.

As for the three sisters, their origins and the prominence of the family meant they would face many barriers in a quest for a fulfilling life. If only they did not so strongly bear the Grenford stamp! Still, with her support and that of her sons, all would be well. She hoped. She prayed.

Time to announce her presence. "Miss Markson, is this a good time for an interruption? I have come to take tea with the young ladies."

کمبل همه چیز برای عشق

Hollystone Hall, December 1812
Eleanor smiled at the family gathered in her private sitting

room. Matilda was pouring the tea, and Frances was carefully carrying each cup to the person for whom it had been prepared. Jessica was sitting on the arm of Aldridge's chair, regaling him with stories about the kitten she had adopted from the kitchen. Cedrica sat quietly, as usual, but the distracted smile and the glow of happiness were new, and her thoughts were clearly on her French chef, whom she had, unless Eleanor missed her guess, kissed in the garden last night.

Jonathan—dear Jonathan, back in England and arriving by surprise on Christmas Eve—was making Jessica laugh with faces he was pulling out of Aldridge's view, though from the quirk in the corner of Aldridge's mouth, he was well aware of his brother's antics.

Eleanor smiled around the room at her children, her heart at ease to have all five of her children with her. Two sons of her body, and three daughters of her heart. Deciding to bring the girls into her nursery had been one of the best decisions she had ever made.

Eleanor accepted another cup of tea from Frances, exchanged a smile with Matilda, and saluted the other three with her cup. How fortunate she was.

If she had been a cowed and obedient wife, her life would have lacked much richness. She had regrets—who didn't? If she'd been braver, she would have permitted the girls to call her 'Mama', rather than 'Aunt Eleanor'. But that would have been a red rag to the duke's bull. The safer path was, probably, the right one.

Eleanor caught Frances's eye and patted the seat beside her. "You did that very well, my dear," she told the girl. Frances was much younger than the other two, and Eleanor was pleased she'd be at home for a while longer. Perhaps, by the time Frances married, one of the others would have given her grandchildren. She smiled again at the thought. Yes, Eleanor had been very fortunate.

EPILOGUE
WINSHIRE HOUSE, LONDON, JANUARY 1813

Eleanor had not visited her friends in Winshire House in nearly a year; had not seen them since they quit London in July, after the series of attacks on the family.

Today, she was going to ignore the prohibitions of the despot who ruled her family. He was convalescing in Kent, and would be away for at least another month. By the time he found out that she had made a condolence call on Grace and Georgie, it would be far too late for him to stop her. She hoped to see her goddaughter, too, who had married James's eldest son just before the turn of the year, a day before the Duke of Winshire died.

At first, she had thought to go on her own, but Matilda and Jessica wanted to express their sympathies to Georgie's daughters, who had been their friends since the cradle. Rather, they seized on the excuse to visit with the girls, whom they had sorely missed during the feud between Haverford and Winshire. No one could possibly imagine that anyone in the Winshire family actually mourned the sour old man who had just died.

Since she was going for precisely the same reason, she agreed, and then Aldridge announced that he planned to escort them.

"When I am duke, Mama, I hope that the new Winshire and I will be able to work together, and I like what I've seen of his sons."

In the end, they all went, late in the afternoon. Only Jon was missing. A month ago, he had sailed from Margate in Aldridge's private yacht, and just this morning, a package had been delivered by a weary sailor, with a report from Aldridge's captain for the marquis, and a brief note from Jon for his mother. "Married. Safe. More news later." Aldridge grinned at the scrawled words. "Jon has landed on his feet again, Mama," he told her. He shook his head, his eyes twinkling. "I don't know how he always manages to do that!"

The Winshire drawing room was crowded, of course, but the Haverfords were invited to remove themselves to a private parlour, where their hostesses joined them after the other visitors had completed the polite fifteen minutes and been shown out.

"Do stay for refreshments," Grace begged, and before long Lord Andrew Winderfield had carried Aldridge off for a game of billiards, the girls from both families had gone up to the twins' little sitting room, and the older ladies settled in to catch up on all that had happened in their lives while they had been separated.

James joined them part way through the conversation, staying when his sister assured him he was not intruding. *I did not come to see him.* Of course, she had not. And yet, here he was and she felt herself turn towards him, a sunflower to his sun. She hoped her reaction was hidden from her friends. *Thank goodness, my all-too-perceptive son is out of the room.*

The new Duke of Winshire. *Had my father accepted his offer for my hand, I would still have become a duchess, in the end.* And there would be no Aldridge. No Jonathan. Perhaps none of the charities she had brought into existence out of her own urge to make the world an easier place for women.

David would still exist, if his grandfather had not beaten him to death in childhood. He'd been conceived before the Duke of Haverford even set eyes on Eleanor.

None of James's wonderful children, though.

Perhaps Matilda, Jessica, and Frances might have been born,

too, though who knew whether they would have survived and what they might have become without her intervention.

As if her thought had conjured them up, the girls came back into the room, and immediately, the Winderfield girls began telling their elders about "Aunt Eleanor's house party to support women's education."

"Matilda and Jessica have been telling us all about it, Papa," the elder of James's daughters told him, perching on the arm of his chair and leaning trustingly against his shoulder. "I want to help girls who want to acquire medical knowledge. What do you think, Papa?"

James looked past his daughter to smile warmly at Eleanor. "Your wards are powerful advocates of your cause, Your Grace." He turned his attention back to his daughter. "Ruth, it is your money to invest. Perhaps you could fund a scholarship?"

The others broke in with objections about finding teachers, and strategies for overcoming that obstacle. Eleanor sat quietly in the warmth of James's smile. Yes, they could be friends. It would be enough. And the charities she had sponsored as Duchess of Haverford would be in safe hands for the next generation. What wonderful daughters her three were.

PART III

PARADISE AT LAST

Long ago, when they were young, James and Eleanor were deeply in love. But their families tore them apart and they went on to marry other people.

Thirty-five years later, they met again. She was Duchess of Haverford and he the Duke of Winshire. Though he was a widower, she was still married. They could only be friends.

Now Haverford is deceased, nothing stands between them. Except that James has not forgiven Eleanor for putting the dynasty of the Haverfords ahead of his niece's happiness.

Can two lovers who are star-crossed again find their happiness at last? Or will their own pride or the villain who wants to destroy the Haverfords stand in their way?

JUDE KNIGHT
Paradise AT Last
The final novella in The Return of the Mountain King
THE DUCHESS AND HER DUKE

To lovers, especially those in their autumn years. Whether you have just found one another, found one another again, or enjoyed being with one another for most of a lifetime, may you future together be as bright as the one I envisage for James and Eleanor.

1

N*ovember 1815*
Eleanor Haverford was bored. Bored, bored, bored. She was tired of wearing dull black; tired of dresses with minimal trim and accessories that repeated the dismal colour. She hated the unspoken rules that restricted the types of activity a widow might enjoy. She missed her friends and her usual social and charitable round.

She was tired of her own company. Two months ago, her secretary had married the local vicar. With many of Eleanor's former tasks now in the hands of the new duchess and her other activities curtailed, she had not bothered to seek a replacement.

She despised the hypocrisy that expected her to make an outward show of mourning a cruel despot who had never shown her a particle of affection or consideration, and who would have consumed every vestige of her will and destroyed all her happiness if she had not found ways to manage him.

She would be honest with herself though she dissembled to the rest of the world. The feeling that currently ruled her life was grief, but not for her husband.

In six months, she had seen James Winshire once, in a crowd, when he came formally with his children and nieces to pay his respects in London after Haverford's funeral. She mourned all the bright possibilities that she had refused to allow herself to consider before Haverford died—the ones that had sparkled in the periphery of her imagination despite her rigid determination not to dishonour her marriage even in thought.

She had not seen her son and his wife in nearly as many months. They had accompanied the coffin to Haverford Castle in the north east of Kent for the interment in the family tomb, but then returned to London. Charlotte, the new duchess, had written to her mother-in-law. The new duke had not. "He has put on his father's coldness with his father's title," she grumbled, but she knew it was not true. Anger, not indifference, prompted his silence. He had not forgiven her for trying to prevent his marriage.

Three months ago, Charlotte had invited Eleanor's wards to join her and the duke in London. "The girls must be bored, and Haverford says that three months of mourning must be all Society can expect when the old duke never acknowledged their existence, let alone his part in it."

Haverford. Hearing her son referred to by the hated name shook her every time.

Charlotte invited Eleanor to come with Jessica and Frances, but Eleanor had not felt ready to face the new duke or Ja— or others in London.

Eleanor had sent them off with her blessing, and now they, too, wrote to her, a letter each a week. Jessica's were full of outings on the arm of her betrothed, the Earl of Colyton. Frances was fifteen, an awkward age to be in Town, too old to be satisfied with ducks at St James Park and too young to join the social round. But also in town were Antonia Wakefield and Daisy Redepenning, family connections and of much the same age. Frances's letters described thrilling excursions with one or more of her governesses and quieter days spent in Haverford or Chirbury House, on theatricals or story writing or painting or some other project that enthralled them for a while and then was put aside.

Eleanor longed to see her children, to hear in person about all their doings. Six months of deep mourning was more than enough.

The letter Eleanor had received this morning repeated Charlotte's invitation. Charlotte and Haverford would not be there. The Prince Regent had asked Haverford to join the British contingent in Paris, and Charlotte was going with him. "Rather than send Jessica and Frances back to Haverford Castle, we wondered if you would consider joining them in London."

Perhaps it was time. No more wallowing. Eleanor had lost a husband she never wanted. She had lost her role as the wife of one of England's most powerful men. Even so, she was still Eleanor Haverford. She had built her own reputation and her place within the ton. She might now be the dowager Duchess of Haverford, but nothing else had changed. The connections she had, the power she could wield in Society through those connections, still belonged to her.

"I need work," she told the empty room. "A project. Something to do to help others." It was time to return to Society.

کمبل همه چیز برای عشق

James, Duke of Winshire, caught himself scanning the ballroom for one face. Whenever he went out in Society, he looked for Eleanor Haverford. Never mind that the dowager duchess had left London immediately after her husband's funeral months ago. Never mind that he was still deeply upset with the way she had tried to prevent the marriage of her son and his niece. Against logic and common sense, he watched for her everywhere. Six months had not dulled the hollow ache of loss at her absence.

London was thin of company this late in the year, with Parliament not in session. A flurry of diplomacy in the wake of the great final battle of Napoleon had brought foreign royals to London, but even visiting archdukes from Austria and a Russian princess had been insufficient to tempt many of the foremost families from their own country estates or house parties at the estates of others.

What entertainments there were generally suffered if they could not boast the attendance of at least one of the visitors. Lady Roscoe's ball was not one of those so favoured, but she had still attracted a good turnout. The great vaulted room was filled with those who lived in the great city all year round or who had business that required them to brave the November slush and fog.

James was there as a favour to the hostess, or at least to her husband, who was wavering on support for a bill to provide help for those being dismissed from the army after injuries acquired in the service of their King.

The usual chattering flock of maidens hovered in his vicinity, trying to attract his attention. In the thirty-three months since he ascended to his title, he'd lost count of the number of ladies who happened to swoon or trip or collapse just as he passed close enough to catch them. Sometimes, he fantasised about speeding up in time to let them crash to the floor behind him. So far, he had resisted the temptation.

At least the marriageable females could be defeated by icy civility. Not so the bored matrons and dashing widows looking for less respectable liaisons. They found it incredible that a widower who was also a wealthy duke might survive without someone to warm his bed, and therefore assumed he was extremely discreet, which made an affair with him even more to be desired.

He had been without a lover for more than a decade, since the death of his beloved wife, Mahzad. Whether they believed it or not, he was not looking for a mistress. As a young man, he had been unusual among his wild friends in needing an emotional connection before he could consider physical intimacy. Since experiencing the heights of bliss and the joys of partnership with Mahzad, he had even less interest in mindless coupling.

Nor did he need a wife. He had his heir; his eldest son whose wife was carrying their second child. Five other sons provided assurance against some dreadful disaster. In all the years since Mahzad's death, he had considered joining his life with only one other. With Eleanor, whom he had lost once again.

Mrs Turner was approaching, a predatory gleam in her eye.

James was pretty sure it was her who had groped his bottom when they stood side by side in the reception line. She stopped when greeted by a friend, and James took the opportunity to step sideways behind a group who were earnestly discussing, of all things, the most fashionable colour to use for evening turbans.

"Avoiding an ambush, Duke?" He knew that amused contralto, and turned to smile at the speaker as she slipped a hand onto his elbow.

"Mrs Kellwood. How are you this evening?" The widow had become a friend in the past few months—a safe lady to spend time with at events such as this. She had, initially, suggested a more intimate relationship, but had readily accepted his refusal.

"I survive, my dear, but would be the better for a stroll on the terrace, if you would be kind enough to oblige me."

James offered his arm, wondering if she was about to overstep the boundaries of friendship, but she made no attempt to press close or to lean on his arm. Still, he stiffened when she admitted, "I have an ulterior motive, Duke. I will tell you all about it when we are out of the crowd."

But all she was after was a listening ear. "My son is insisting I invest in this mining venture, Duke, and—I don't know. I can see nothing wrong with it, but I just have a feeling..." She shrugged. "Am I being foolish? Do you know anything about diamond mining in the Cape Colony?

James's guilt at having ascribed to her, even briefly, the marital or lustful motives of so many other females had him offering to read the prospectus and ask a few quiet questions among his contacts.

"I could not ask you!" she exclaimed. "You are so busy."

James hastened to assure her that it would be no trouble; that he would be pleased to help out a friend.

She conceded gracefully. "It is very kind of you, and I am sure that it is not at all what you planned for tomorrow afternoon, but if you would call upon me—perhaps around two in the afternoon? I would be so relieved to be able to show the papers to you and get your opinion."

She then insisted on going inside, pointing out that they did not want to start tongues wagging. Quite right, too. It was so restful to have a lady who was just a friend and wanted nothing from him he was not willing to give.

2

The sun was setting by the time Eleanor's carriage and outriders arrived at Haverford House on the outskirts of London. Weather had made a nightmare of the trip from Haverford Castle, which was far to the east near Margate in Kent. Slowed by torrential rain and the resulting mud, slips, washed out roads and floods, they had spent three nights in inns—two more than intended.

But they were here at last. Eleanor was eager to see Frances and Jessica, and hear how they were and what they'd been doing. "While I am visiting with Miss Frances and Miss Jessica, Fletcher, please order a hot bath for me," she told her dresser. "And one for yourself, as well. You have travelled as far as I." Her carriage was well-sprung and comfortable, but even the most luxurious seating left one stiff and sore after four days of travel over rutted roads.

"I will see to you first, Your Grace," Fletcher promised.

Eleanor shook her head. "I intend to eat my dinner in my room and in a banyan, so I will not require you again this evening after you have settled my things in my room." She leaned forward to step out of the carriage, taking the hand her groom extended to her.

Tired as she was, she had forgotten about the retirement of the butler who had served her when she was chatelaine here. His replacement hurried down the main steps with an umbrella to hold over her head, a footman following with another for her dresser. "Richards," she greeted the man, whom she had known since he was a child on one of the Haverford estates. "How are you? How are you finding your new role?"

"Wonderful, Your Grace. A well-trained staff is a joy to direct."

Eleanor turned from him to farewell her coachman, groom, and outriders. "Find your beds as soon as you may," she ordered. "You have served me well."

The butler escorted her inside, with the footman and Fletcher following behind. "And may one ask after Your Grace?" he asked. "How was your travel in this awful weather?"

They chatted for a moment in the magnificent entrance hall, Eleanor giving part of her mind to the conversation while noting small differences. A different carpet before the massive fireplace, a pair of large vases that had once adorned the ballroom now on pedestals either side of the door that led to the duke's offices. Minor things, but an added reminder that the Haverford houses now had a new mistress.

"I will go up to Miss Frances and Miss Jessica first, Richards. Are they in their rooms?"

Richards shook his head. "No, Your Grace. Miss Frances has been staying with the Chirburys since their graces left for Paris. Their graces took Miss Jessica with them, and the duchess thought that Miss Frances would be lonely without any of the family in residence."

"Yes, quite right," Eleanor managed to say, with outward calm, though inwardly she reeled. Jessica had gone to Paris? And they had not asked Eleanor first? *How silly of me. She is an adult and does not need my permission to travel.* Indeed, she would be married the next year. *But Frances is still my ward, and I expected her to be here.*

She thrust back the spurt of sour anger, embarrassed at her petty resentment at being superseded. Frances was better off staying with Daisy Chirbury rather than alone with only the servants for company. *Still is, for I shall no doubt be busy. Ald— Haverford and Charlotte only made the decision I would have made.*

"I shall have to visit the Chirburys tomorrow then. I will write a note, Richards. Can you arrange for someone to deliver it tonight? I know the weather is dreadful."

Richards bowed. "Of course, Your Grace." He allowed himself a slight twitch of the lips that was not quite a smile. "None of our footmen melt. Is there anything else you require?"

She rewarded his joke with a smile of her own. "Perhaps a light supper sent up to my rooms in about an hour. I intend an early night."

But Fletcher had stopped part way up the stairs, looking back at them with her brows drawn into a frown. "What suite has Her Grace been given, Mr Richards?" she asked.

Ah yes. Of course. It should have occurred to her, but it had not. She had been about to ascend to the traditional chambers of the Duchess of Haverford—an entire suite of rooms that mirrored and were adjacent to the duke's suite.

Another reminder that she was no longer the mistress of this house and the other houses of the ducal estates.

As was only right and proper. Her son had succeeded to the titles and estates, and his wife had taken Eleanor's place as Duchess of Haverford, chatelaine to his houses, hostess of his entertainments, supporter of his ambitions, and advocate for his petitioners.

She could easily be one of those petitioners herself, dependent on the goodwill of Haverford and his duchess, except that she had received good advice over the years and had invested what she could of her stipend, to which she now added her dower. She could live out her days in material comfort without relying on her son, and six months ago had feared that would be her fate. But he was minded to be generous, it seemed. Or Charlotte was.

Charlotte, she decided, as she stepped inside the suite prepared for her to use. It had been redecorated in Eleanor's favourite colours, and the furnishings she had loved best had all been moved for her continued enjoyment. There, over the mantel of the fire-place, was the painting of Aldridge and Jonathan as young boys, which had graced her sitting room for the past twenty-two years, since it left the artist's hands.

Her favourite chairs were pulled up by the fireplace, and—she walked over to touch them and check—had been recovered in a fabric so close to the original they looked just as they had when she had first chosen them.

Another set of chairs and sofa were grouped near the window, ready for guests. Charlotte had gone a step further and recreated a feature Eleanor had admired in her goddaughter Sophia's rooms at Winds' Gate, the Winshire family estate. There, in the window, was a built-in reading nook, a comfortable window seat lined at each end with bookshelves.

The door on one side of the sitting room led into a reproduction of the study she had created in the duchess's rooms, with her writing desk placed where the light from the window would fall over her shoulder.

The other door led to the bedchamber. Again, Charlotte had taken pains to use familiar furnishings and colours, and to enhance with the painting and ornaments that were either Eleanor's own or that she had used for so long that she felt she had come home.

Fletcher came out of the dressing room, wreathed in smiles. "Camphor chests and shelves," she reported. "We shall be very comfortable here, Your Grace."

Perhaps they would. Certainly, Eleanor's heart felt lighter. *Perhaps Aldr— or rather, Haverford as I must call him now—is softening towards me.* From that thought, her heart leapt to James and she quelled it sternly. She was here in London to be reunited with her fosterling Frances, to spend some time with her friends, to find out what good she might be able to do in the world now that her time was her own, and to see her son and his wife when they returned from Paris.

That was quite enough to be going on with.

کمبل همه چیز برای عشق

Mrs Kellwood lived on the same square as the London residence of the Chirburys, though on the north-facing side in a row of much smaller town houses than Chirbury House and its companion mansions.

James could see the more impressive side of the square from the pretty little room Mrs Kellwood called her library, though it had only one small book case and a pretty writing desk too small for much beyond letter writing, and was otherwise appointed as a ladies' withdrawing room. He kept sneaking glances out of the window, for the coach being walked up and down in front of the opposite row of houses bore the Haverford crest.

No doubt it was there to drop off or collect Miss Frances Grenford, who was a friend of the earl's daughter. Though it seemed a very formal coach for transporting a schoolgirl and her governess.

He wrenched his mind back to the papers Mrs Kellwood had spread before him, declaring her ignorance with self-deprecating grace, but pointing to several paragraphs that she said made her uncomfortable. "Either I don't understand them, Duke," she said, "or they are not at all to my advantage."

He tended to agree with discomfort. "You may be right, Mrs Kellwood," he told her. "I have asked a couple of questions on your behalf, and have several more now that I have seen the proposal. May I meet with you tomorrow and tell you what I have discovered?"

"I would be very grateful," the lady assured him. "Now. You must let me reward you. I have a brandy that I think you would find palatable, or would you prefer something else?" She glanced out the window, and James hoped she hadn't noticed his lapses of attention.

He stood, preparing to refuse her invitation and make his farewells, but she had crossed to a set of decanters and was pouring from one of them into two glasses. "Just a small one, then," he said. She was right. It was a pleasant brandy, and deserved to be savoured.

They chatted idly while they warmed their glasses with their hands. Mrs Kellwood didn't sit again, but crossed to stand by the window, so James stood with her, asking about her plans for the coming week, and whether she intended to retreat to the country now that Parliament was in recess and the foreign dignitaries whose visits had so entertained the masses had scattered out to various grand estates.

Suddenly, Mrs Kellwood put down her glass, saying, "Merciful heavens, is that the time? Winshire, I shall have to hurry you, I fear, though I am very rude to do so when you are doing me such a favour."

James put his own empty glass by hers. "I was about to take my leave, so you are not hurrying me at all." He followed her into the entry hall, where the butler stood already holding his hat and coat. A maid hurried downstairs with Mrs Kellwood's bonnet and cloak, and helped her mistress don them while James put on his own outdoor wear.

"Are you going far?" he asked. "Can I call you a hackney?"

"Just to the end of the row," she assured him. "I shall walk, and be better for the fresh air."

"Then I shall escort you, and my man will follow with my horse." One of his younger retainers was walking his own mount and James's Xander up and down the street outside.

James offered Mrs Kellwood his arm as they descended her front steps, just as the Haverford carriage approached around the square. James looked up into Eleanor's eyes. He doffed his hat with a slight bow. She inclined her head in reply, and then they were passed.

"The Duchess of Haverford is back in town," Mrs Kellwood observed. "Was that Lord Redepenning with her?"

James hadn't noticed. "Quite likely. Her carriage was outside the Chirburys. I daresay Lord Henry was, too—he is related to the earl."

Mrs Kellwood nodded. "As is Her Grace. I daresay they met there, then. They have always been good friends, of course, and now that Her Grace is a widow... But one must not speculate. I abhor gossip of all things. Do you not agree, duke?"

His agreement was absent. He was still wondering if there was any truth in her idle remark. *Eleanor and Henry?* Surely not! Though it was none of his business, of course. Still, when he had seen Mrs

Kellwood to her destination, he turned to look after the carriage, now disappearing down Wynde Street, more unsettled than he wished to acknowledge.

کمبل همه چیز برای عشق

"I did not realise that the Duke of Winshire was a close acquaintance of Mrs Kellwood," Eleanor commented. *An intimate acquaintance? Perhaps. He had certainly emerged from her house well before the usual visiting hours.* She wrestled with the hot jealousy that attempted to escape her iron control. *It is none of my business. James and I have—had —no understanding. Especially not after...*

Henry, Baron Redepenning, leaned closer to the window to watch the couple strolling down the street together, Mrs Kellwood clinging to James's arm. "They are much in one another's company at balls and concerts and the like, but I have not heard of an affair," he said.

Not consoling. If James had taken the woman as a lover, he would be careful of her reputation, though leaving by her front door in full daylight was hardly inconspicuous. Did that mean they were not lovers? *It is none of your business, Eleanor,* she scolded herself.

She had encountered Henry at Chirbury House when she called to collect Frances. Frances had greeted her with enthusiasm, but was less delighted at the idea of returning to Haverford House.

She, Daisy, Antonia, and a couple of other acquaintances had a full timetable of activities planned, "And very little time to complete them all, Aunt Eleanor," Frances had explained, "since Daisy is leaving London at the end of the week to go back to Gloucestershire. Coming home would mean extra time travelling every day, and I would miss out on all the fun in the evenings. I may stay, may I not?"

The upshot was that Eleanor left without Frances, but with Henry, whom she had offered to drop at the headquarters of the Horse Guard where he had his office, on her way back to Haverford House.

On second thoughts, she might call on a couple of other

acquaintances while she was out. Her niece-in-law, Anne Chirbury, had mentioned a few people who were in town, and had talked about the difficulties facing the country-folk after a succession of poor harvests during the war, and high prices for grain. Henry was concerned for the injured and sick soldiers and sailors who were still trickling home from foreign ports after the tragedy that was Waterloo ended the long war with France.

Surely Cedrica Fournier would be home, and she would have a different perspective on the problems facing Londoners, since she lived here all year round, and she and her husband owned a successful restaurant.

None of the Winderfield women were in town, though Eleanor would, in any case, be reluctant to call on James's family without a direct invitation. But Henry had mentioned that the Earl of Hythe had arrived back from Vienna, and his sister, Lady Felicity Belvoir, had co-operated with Eleanor on several philanthropic causes. She could think of one or two others, too.

By the end of the afternoon, she had met with five of the women she had worked with before, three in high society and two with a firmer finger on the pulse of the merchant ranks of Society. All of them had causes to espouse, and all of them were doing something about it.

"I learned from the best, Aunt Eleanor," said Cedrica, who was a distant cousin and had once been Eleanor's secretary. "I see a need and figure out how to bring it to the attention of others, as you taught me."

The other women repeated variations on the same theme. They credited Eleanor with the inspiration, which was kind of them, but the fact was they were doing very well without her. When they realised she was looking for work, they all suggested roles for her. And all of the roles were minor, and could have been done by anyone.

In penance for her pique at that thought, she accepted every task she was offered. At least she would be busy for the few weeks until Haverford and Charlotte returned from Paris, and they all retired to the country.

3

Eleanor suddenly seemed to be everywhere James went. She was seeking support for several philanthropic projects, by all accounts, though she did not approach James.

"It must be difficult," said Mrs Kellwood, "for her to take a back seat when she has been accustomed to leading—or at least being the patroness—of the charities she has favoured with her attention."

James nodded. "Yes, you are right. It is to her credit that she is stepping back and allowing others the lead role. Of course, she has always cared about the causes she supports more than her own aggrandisement. It is one of the things one can admire about her."

"It is," Mrs Kellwood agreed. "And such a diversity, too. Injured soldiers. Starving weavers. Teaching seamstresses to read and write. Slaves in the Caribbean. One wonders at the common thread."

James didn't wonder. "They are all in need," he explained. "She has a big heart."

"I expect you are right," Mrs Kellwood said. "I daresay that also explains the involvement of Lord Redepenning, whose compassion for others is well known. And he has long been a friend of the dowager's, of course. I suppose that must be true of Mr Tolliver, too, for if Lord Redepenning is not her escort, Mr Tolliver is, though no-one seems to know who he is or what he does."

Most of the upper *ton* knew that Tolliver ran some shadowy department in the Home Office. Only those in inner government circles also knew, as James did, that the man was responsible for much shadowy government work, both in the United Kingdom and beyond its shores.

James frowned at Tolliver. Very few people would be able to name his antecedents—his true name was Fitzgrenford, and he was a base-born half-brother to Eleanor's deceased husband.

A secret that might be better kept if the man did not pat the duchess's hand in such a familiar manner, smiling at her with a warmth James had seldom seen from the cold and distant man. Another suitor? Surely not. Tolliver was like a brother to her. Wasn't he?

Mrs Kellwood made another remark about Lord Henry, or Lord Redepenning, as she insisted on calling him. He had been knighted as a young man, and had been Sir Henry for so long that, when the King awarded him a barony, his intimates switched to calling him Lord Henry, and it stuck.

Further evidence of her marginal status in Society.

James scolded himself for his aristocratic arrogance. The assumption held by most of his class that they were inherently superior to all other mortals had always rankled, and he was disturbed to catch elements of it in himself.

In fact, one of the reasons he liked Mrs Kellwood was that she did not pretend to greet his lightest pronouncement as if it had been handed down from Mt Sinai, engraved on stone. Unlike so many of the widows who lived on the periphery of Society. He despised those who treated him with exaggerated deference.

And her pretty gratitude for his help was gratifying. He had advised against the canal investment, and suggested another.

He was concerned about causing a breach between mother and son, but when he bumped into young Kellwood and discussed the matter with him, Kellwood took the stand that he'd never promoted the canal scheme. Embarrassed to have urged his mother into something that was poorly thought through, presumably. James let the matter drop, pleased he'd been able to assist the lady.

"He is known to be in the confidence of Her Grace the dowager duchess," Mrs Kellwood commented. James had to hunt back through the conversation to realise she meant Tolliver. "Yes," he answered absently, as he watched Eleanor laughing at something Lord Henry said. They certainly seemed very comfortable with one another.

Then she looked his way and the laughter died. She inclined her head and he nodded in response.

Mrs Kellwood's voice came as if from a distance. "Are you planning to visit the opera, duke? Angelina Bianci is singing Figaro next week. Her European tour was very well regarded."

A sliver of caution insinuated itself into his regard for the lady, though he kept his voice neutral as he answered. "I had not thought to do so." He was waiting in town for the arrival of his son Andrew. Drew was returning from a trip to Sardinia, where he met with another of James's sons, John, who operated the family's merchant fleet and their trading operations in the Mediterranean, and through the Black Sea into Northern Europe. He'd received a message only this morning that Drew's ship was docked in Calais, and that he expected to be in London within the next forty-eight hours.

"Oh, but you must!" Mrs Kellwood insisted. "You have a box, do you not? If you do not wish to go alone, you could get up a party."

With her as part of it, presumably. Or perhaps he was meant to suggest that she was the only company he needed. Or perhaps her remark was entirely innocent and James had become top lofty and conceited, looking for ulterior motives in every woman he met.

"I am afraid I won't be able to attend the Opera, Mrs Kellwood. I will be leaving for my country estate as soon as my son Drew returns to England, which will be tomorrow or the next day."

He glanced over towards Eleanor again. Tomorrow was Thursday, long established as the day that they had met in secret if they were both in London. If he called in at Miss Clemens Book Emporium and Tea Shop, and asked for the key to the Paeony Room under the name of Mr Traveller, would she be there?

He wouldn't do it. Eleanor wouldn't be there. She knew how disgusted he was at the way she interfered in the romance of her son and his niece. James could not abide manipulative women.

Mrs Kellwood was making a little moue. "How flat London shall be without you. Are you sure…? But I must not badger you. Of course, you have obligations to your family that a mere friend cannot disarrange."

"Indeed," James agreed, and there it was. A flash of irritation, quickly masked. Mrs Kellwood was perhaps not as safe a lady or as good a friend as she pretended. Just as well that James was retreating to the country—a physical distance as a prelude to their future emotional distance.

"And with that in mind, Mrs Kellwood, I must take my leave of you. If I do not see you again before I leave London, may I wish you all the best of the holiday season? Do you go to your son?"

"I do." The lady gave a shudder of distaste, then gathered her smile and her manners. "My best wishes to you and your family."

James bowed, and walked away, trying not to hurry. He did not like manipulative women.

کمبل همه چیز برای عشق

On Thursday, Eleanor sat in the Paeony Room writing letters. She had offered to approach potential donors for money for an infirmary for the poor and indigent. She had promised the chair of the fundraising committee to send fifty letters by the end of the week.

Each had to be crafted to the addressee—all ladies of high-estate with enough pin money to give generously or sympathetic husbands who could be persuaded to support the cause. A personal appeal from a duchess, even a dowager duchess, was unlikely to be refused.

Her mind was not on the task, however. She kept listening for footsteps outside the door, but when they came, they always passed. Before she chose this particular place for her letter writing, she had told herself that James would not come. She would be there, just on the remote chance. But she would bring her work and would not expect him.

But apparently, she had lied to herself. Her body's reactions told her that, deep down, she had believed he would join her—the lightness each time she heard someone outside the door, the way her heart swooped into her belly when the person did not enter.

After an hour, hope had died. He had not forgiven her. He would not even give her the courtesy of a hearing. After an hour and a half, she had completed fifteen letters. She blotted the last one, folded it, sealed it and addressed it. It joined the others in the bag she had brought for the purpose. It was time to go.

Three days later, she heard that the Duke of Winshire had left for Winds' Gate. So that was it, then. He intended to make no move to bridge the divide between them. Very well, then. She had built a perfectly tolerable life for herself for thirty-five years after the first time she lost him. She could do it again.

4

Charlotte wrote from Paris asking if the family could all gather at Hollystone Hall for Christmas, the letter reaching Eleanor only a couple of days before her return with Haverford and Jessica.

Hollystone Hall was a day's travel from London and a day or two at the most from those members of the family who were already at their country estates. It was no longer part of the Haverford holdings. The lovely Tudor manor had been part of Eleanor's dowry, and became her property on the death of her husband.

It had always been a favourite retreat, and she wrote back immediately to give her consent. Perhaps in the relaxed atmosphere of Hollystone Hall, she could mend the breach between her and her son.

He was distant but polite on his return, and continued so through the first days of the house party, as the family gathered. Eleanor found herself monitoring his movements and his mood, always from a distance.

It was a skill she had honed through the purgatory of her marriage. She used to move from conversation to conversation around the room, her social personality firmly in place, trying to stay at least two groups away from the previous Haverford, trying not to attract his attention when forced into his presence.

But her son was not his father. Physically, they were very much alike. Like his father at a similar age, her son was tall, with broad shoulders tapering to a lean waist and hips, and the thighs of a horseman. They shared some facial features, though she fancied her son took his chin from her side of the family. He had his father's colouring, too: fair hair, pale English skin that pinked rapidly in the sun, and hazel eyes.

It was the eyes that hinted at what different men they were. When the new duke let down his social armour in the company of family, and his eyes lit with humour and affection, no one could mistake him for the cold tyrant who had sired him.

He was treating her with the manners he offered to a stranger. It was her own fault. Even at the time, Eleanor had known she was wrong to try to persuade Charlotte to refuse his proposal. She had thought her reasons were sound. A minor motive was to avoid the scandal if Charlotte's secret sorrow was made public, as indeed it was. She had not expected her son to stand by Charlotte through the mess that followed. She was wrong. Apparently, he already knew most of it, and didn't care about the rest.

More important than that, she feared what would become of Charlotte if the doctors were right, and the girl was barren. She had assumed that he would want to follow the Haverford tradition of passing the title father to son in a straight line all the way back to the family's founder. Her opinion had been tainted by her own experience during the years she failed to provide a second son to ensure the line. Her Haverford had grown colder and colder, more and more furious. Even though he already had his heir. Even though he had given her the disease that contributed to two miscarriages and a stillbirth. It was her job to give him a backup son for the heir she had already produced, and she had failed.

Her son scoffed at the family tradition, and claimed that Charlotte as his wife was all that he needed and desired. It was early days. They had only been married for a few months. However, she was beginning to believe him. For her third and most important reason had been thoroughly debunked. She thought his history as a rake proved his inability to be faithful to one woman beyond that first wild infatuation.

She did not doubt that Charlotte loved Aldridge, as he was then. Or, at least, that she was well on the way to doing so. But she had ignored the two-year absence of credible gossip about his affairs. She thought he had simply become more discreet as he took on more and more of the ducal responsibilities. She would have trusted his word if he had told her that, despite Charlotte's third refusal of his proposal in 1812, he had decided to be faithful to her while he worked to change her mind. Two years!

Perhaps, if Eleanor had known that, she would still have believed his love would fade. Even though he told Charlotte he had not even been tempted, that she was the only woman he wanted, she might have dismissed it as nonsense.

After all, his father seldom gave up on an infatuation while in the heat of a chase. Having won his prize, he lost interest in it.

She was wrong again. Nearly eight months after their wedding, the love between Haverford and Charlotte had grown—or Cherry, as she was now known, the rest of the family adopting Haverford's name for her. They showed it in a thousand ways. Glances across a room. Little touches. Shared smiles. Warm looks. A preference for one another's company. If they were separated for any length of time—and to them an hour was a length of time—one of them would find a reason to go in search of the other. They even shared a study. In London, the old duke's desk and the little one Haverford had used when he was Aldridge had both been removed. The window nook now held two desks of equal size, a his and hers.

She owed her son an apology. She had already acknowledged her wrong-doing to Cherry, and been forgiven. But how could she tell her son of her remorse when he avoided her, and spoke to her only with distant politeness?

She would have to ask him for a private audience, but before she nerved herself to do so, he made the request himself. She followed him to the library, and allowed him to close the door behind them.

She spoke before he had the opportunity. "Haverford, I have

apologised for interfering between you and Cherry, but I would like to do so again. I have known all along that I was wrong to go privately to Cherry as I did. You are adults, and I should have said what I thought to both of you and trusted you to make your own decision. I am truly sorry for the distress I caused you."

Haverford opened his mouth, but before he could speak, Eleanor put up a hand to stop him. "I have a second apology to make, Haverford. Watching you and Cherry together in the past week shows me that I was wrong again—wrong to believe that your love for Cherry was less deep than hers for you. Wrong to think that you would fall out of love once you had achieved your prize. All I ever wanted was for both of you to be happy. You are perfect for one another, and I shudder to think how close I came to preventing the very happiness I sought to protect."

For a moment, Haverford said nothing, his mouth hanging slightly open as if the words he'd planned to say had dissolved on his tongue. Then he gave a slight shake of his head. "Thank you, Mama."

"I will never interfere again," Eleanor promised. *Perhaps that was a bit rash.* "At least, I will try my very best."

Haverford's smile was small, but it reached his eyes. "I shall not ask such a sacrifice, Mama. Both Cherry and her mother have pointed out what a marvellous gift you have for interfering, as you call it. All I ask is that you consult us first on any plans you have that involve us and that you promise not to proceed without our agreement."

Eleanor's eyes were wet. She blinked to clear them. "I can promise that, Haverford," she agreed.

He looked down at his hands, and a slight colour rose in his cheeks. "It sounds odd when my own mother calls me that name. Could you bring yourself to call me Anthony, do you think?"

Eleanor blinked back tears. "Truly? Oh, yes, Haver… Anthony. I would be grateful for that privilege."

He smiled, just a little. "It is my name, after all. Just between family."

She managed a small joke. "En famille it will be, my son. It would not do to rock the foundations of Society!"

His smile broadened. "Come on, Mama. We have a house to decorate."

He offered her his hand to help her rise, and his elbow to escort her back to the ballroom, just in time to see a footman moving a ladder away from the arched doorway. A kissing ball hung in the middle of the arch. Cherry stood looking up at it, and she glanced their way and smiled to see them together.

Haverford put his arm around Eleanor, reached up for a mistletoe berry, and pressed a gentle kiss to her cheek. "I love you, Mama," he told her. "Merry Christmas."

And it was.

5

E *arly February 1816*
"I see the Haverfords are back in town," said Viscountess Woollam. Before she and her friends had descended on them, James had been talking to her husband about the government's proposal to continue the income tax imposed during the war with France. Woollam was older than James by at least a decade, and had married the former Baroness Thirby in somewhat mysterious circumstances at the end of last season. His wife was half his age, and the worst kind of fashionable vixen. She had threaded her hand into James's arm, so he could not easily leave without outright rudeness. He was near the point of employing it.

In the long and boring minutes that followed, she and those with her had shredded several reputations, critiqued the gowns of most of the attractive women in the ballroom, and mocked the characters of the most notable men.

James had nearly stopped listening before the comment about the Haverfords captured his wandering attention. He turned to watch the duke descend the steps to the ballroom, his mother on his left arm and his wife on his right, while his sister followed on the arm of her betrothed, the Earl of Colyton.

"Her Grace doesn't look well," Lady Woollam observed. "Perhaps marriage does not agree with her."

"I wonder why they are back in town?" That was one of the viscountess's cicisbeos—Matthew something. A pup with a lace cravat and a deliberate lisp. James didn't bother to enlighten the fool. Parliament was back in session, and the Duke of Haverford was scrupulous about fulfilling his obligations.

"I daresay His Grace is already neglecting the poor dear," Lady Woollam cooed, her feigned sympathy curdled by her glare at the young duchess. "If she had asked me…" Mrs Meecham, who was never far from the viscountess's side, grasped her friend's arm. "Margaret!" she warned, casting a glance at James, the young duchess's uncle.

Lord Woollam was turning puce at his wife's maladroit poison. James took Lady Woollam's hand and removed it from his arm. He bowed to Woollam, pointedly ignoring the viscountess and her pack. "Perhaps we can continue our discussion when we are not in company, my lord. I must greet my niece and her husband."

He crossed the floor to the Haverfords, leaving silence behind him.

Eleanor looked to be in the pink of health. The lines of strain had faded from around her eyes, which were smiling again as she looked at her son and his wife. The smile vanished when she caught him looking. She pressed her lips tightly together before composing her face into a bland mask.

He quashed the urge to say that he was sorry. Devil take it. He had done nothing to apologise for. Apart from leaving her waiting for more than an hour at the Paeony Room in December. He had called at the bookshop earlier this week, and Miss Clemens, the proprietor, had managed to work that little fact into the conversation. All the time Eleanor had been waiting, he had been in his study fifteen minutes brisk walk away, telling himself over and over that she had made their previous arrangement null and void when she hurt his niece.

That was still true, even if she and the two most seriously affected appeared to have resolved their differences.

After polite greetings, he was pleased that she strolled away to greet friends, less delighted that she did so on the arm of Lord Henry. Perhaps the long-time widower was looking for another wife?

James was disgusted at his own irritation. Clearly his instincts regarding Eleanor had not caught up with the facts. Once he had thought… but that was before. She and Henry Redepenning were both unattached, and if they thought of a future together, then he should wish them well.

Lord Colyton took Jessica dancing, and Charlotte fell into a conversation with a friend. James, in a determined effort not to look around the ballroom to see whether Eleanor and Henry had remained inside, asked Haverford about his thoughts on the matters currently before Parliament, and soon they were exchanging opinions. For the most part, they saw eye to eye, though Haverford thought it too soon to cancel the income tax imposed nearly twenty years earlier to fund the war, and James was in favour of relieving the burden on merchants, tradespeople, and manufacturers.

Eleanor walked past, deep in conversation with another lady of the same mature years. Henry was nowhere to be seen. James dragged his mind back to the conversation with Haverford, then found himself wondering whether he should visit the Paeony Room this coming Thursday.

What was that? Haverford had said a name James had not expected to hear. "Excuse me. My attention drifted for a moment. Did you say 'Elspeth Ashbury'?" The former countess turned brothelkeeper had been exiled last year, after bartering with information about her villainous brother for immunity from punishment for her part in his evil plots and passage away from England.

Haverford nodded. "Dead. Knifed in a street market in Kingston. It happened around six months ago, but she and her companion were travelling under assumed names and it has taken the investigator Wakefield sent some time to find where she went when she left the ship we put her on."

"The companion?" James asked.

"Disappeared. The port authorities found him guilty in absentia. Wakefield's man considers it unlikely. We know her brother sent an assassin after her before he died, and the description of the lover matches the boy she had with her when she escaped. Kit, his name was."

He shrugged. "Those who witnessed the murder swore the assailant was a second man, and that her lover was distraught, so it appears that Stanley Wharton's assassin finally caught up with her." Haverford shrugged. "In any case, she is gone. I dare say you'll be receiving Wakefield's report, or at least Ashbury will, since she was his sister-in-law."

James considered the news. "It will be a relief to him, I imagine. All told, she and her brother caused much trouble for my family and yours over the past few years. With both of them dead, we can put them out of our mind."

There was Eleanor again, this time with Tolliver. He seldom appeared at entertainments such as this, but in impeccable evening attire, he did not stand out, apart from the company he kept.

Suddenly, he longed for his own library and a glass of his own brandy. Perhaps one of his children might be home and willing to play chess with him. He made his excuses to Haverford, his farewells to his host and hostess, and departed the ball.

کمبل همه چیز برای عشق

For weeks, Eleanor watched from across the crowded rooms of the ton as James was ardently pursued by matrons for their daughters and widows for themselves. His discomfort, carefully concealed under his usual gentle courtesy, gave her no pleasure.

Indeed, with her year of mourning more than three quarters done, she was beginning to encounter her own harassment, even though she was a woman in her fifties. What was it about the denizens of the Beau Monde that they could not see a wealthy widower or widow without desiring to change that state?

The would-be suitors themselves—hungry for wealth, status, or connections—were bad enough. Even her friends could not be trusted to leave the question of matrimony strictly alone. They seemed to think that she should plunge again into the marital waters from which she had only just escaped.

Given that the question of a new duchess for the Duke of Winshire was a favourite topic in every parlour, ballroom, tea shop, and fashionable promenade, she could only assume that possible husbands for the dowager Duchess of Haverford were likewise being discussed and ranked by those same gossips.

Yes, and in the men's clubs and other fashionable male preserves, where the men prattled about other people's business quite as much as their female counterparts.

Henry protected her somewhat. A widower with no interest in changing his state, he was happy to lend her his presence to discourage at least some of the jackanapes who hoped to take her generous settlements and her private fortune into their custody. Dear Tolly, too, was entering Society more often than usual to give her his support. Although, knowing Tolly, there was undoubtedly some matter of State that also required his presence.

Of course, if Cherry and Haverford were attending the same evenings entertainments as Eleanor, her son's escort was her preference. She raised no further gossip that way. However, they had cut back on their outings. Cherry was particularly tired, often ill in the mornings, and glowing with that particular aura produced by women who knew that the evidence of a happy and fruitful marriage was growing within them. The couple had not told Eleanor that Cherry was with child, and she had said nothing to them. But the signs were all there, not least the way Haverford hovered, treating Cherry with tender and reverent care.

He would always escort Eleanor if she asked. She didn't; his clear preference was to be at home with his wife.

How wonderful that the mournful prognostications of the doctors who had treated Cherry so long ago had proved to be entirely wrong.

Eleanor was too busy to fret much about her would-be suitors, or about the chill distance between her and the one man for whom she might be tempted to forsake her new freedom. She and Jessica had much to do preparing for Jessica's wedding in April and shopping for Jessica's trousseau. She continued the work she had begun, seeking donations for the several charities she had offered to help when last in Town.

She also found herself deputising for Cherry on many of the same committees that she had managed when she was duchess. Eleanor met with her daughter-in-law after every meeting to report on progress.

They took tea one afternoon in the little parlour Cherry had made her own. The previous evening Haverford had escorted them both to a formal dinner, with dancing afterwards, at the home of Lord Henry's daughter Susan.

"You will be able to take up the work again, now that you are feeling more energetic," Eleanor told her daughter-in-law. "I'm very happy to hand it all back to you, or to continue with some of it. You must just tell me what you need."

"We shall see," Cherry commented. "I expect I will need your help later in the year. You have guessed have you not?"

Eleanor acknowledged the truth of that with a smile and a nod.

"I thought so. You have not fussed over me as much as Anthony, but you are always there with a snack or a drink when I need it, and always ready to take over when a nap overwhelms me." She put a hand over Eleanor's and squeezed. "You and Mother are the only ones to know, apart from Anthony."

"And, I imagine, your dresser," Eleanor joked. "It is hard to keep such a secret from one's maid."

It was Cherry's turn to smile and nod.

"Dearest, I could not be more thrilled," Eleanor said. "And not because of that nonsense about an heir to the Haverford duchy. I have seen enough of you together to know that the love you bear one another is far more important than who carries on the title after we are all gone. But you deserve the little blessing you carry. You and my son will be wonderful parents."

Cherry burst into tears. "Excuse me, Aunt Eleanor. I seem to have little control over my emotions at the moment." She put her arms around Eleanor and Eleanor hugged her back, then offered a handkerchief so she could dry her eyes.

"And what of you?" Cherry asked. "I always thought you and Uncle James would make a match of it after the old duke died. We would all be so pleased. Can you not talk to him, Aunt Eleanor?"

Eleanor shook her head. "I expect you know what he thinks of me. Sarah was there when he found out what I had done. I cannot even blame him for it, for I was wrong."

Cherry made an impatient noise. "And I suppose he has never made a mistake in his life? To throw away all of your history and the friendship you have found in the last few years—surely he is not so foolish."

Eleanor sighed. "Shall we talk about something else, my dear? What dreadful weather we are having."

6

James had become adept at avoiding marital traps. He could not always prevent an enterprising maiden from tripping into his arms or fainting in his direction, but he could make sure never to be in a room in any house except his own without at least one witness who could be trusted to tell the truth.

The public adulation was nearly as wearying as the private harassment. At least Mrs Kellwood, despite her ulterior motives, didn't pretend that every word he spoke was the most interesting and exciting utterance ever known to womankind.

One afternoon in February, he came home seeking refuge after two young women had accidentally tripped right into him and an importunate widow had hidden in his carriage, to be found and ejected by Yousef before James entered.

The sound of female chatter from the drawing room set his hackles on end, but he relaxed when Grosvenor, the butler, explained that Lady Rosemary was having tea with her sister, Lady Ashbury, and her cousin, the Duchess of Haverford.

James entered the drawing room to greet his daughters and niece, and found his own sister Georgie and her friend Letty were also present. "Georgie! I did not know you were coming up to town!

Welcome! And you, too, Letty. You are both looking very well. How did you find travel in this appalling weather?"

They chatted about the weather, and then about Georgie's reason for the expedition to Town. "Letty has some concerts she'd like to attend, and we both need to refresh our wardrobes."

"And we will be attending a few balls and other events while we are here," Letty added, firmly, laughing at Georgie's grimace. "You know you will enjoy catching up with old friends," she told her.

"Good," James said. "You will allow me the honour of escorting you."

"Our father is being hounded by the marriage minded," Ruth explained to the two new arrivals.

"The girls are bad enough," James confirmed. "But their mothers! And the widows. One hid in my carriage today, and Yousef had the devil of a job—I beg your pardon, ladies—a difficult task ejecting her without attracting the very crowd she wanted to force my hand. Not that it would have. But we did not wish to damage her reputation by publicly showing her up for the designing hussy she is."

"You are a single duke possessed of vast wealth and all your teeth," Georgie pointed out. "You must expect them to be interested."

"They were never this bad before," he complained.

"Because everyone assumed that you were waiting for Eleanor, James," Georgie told him.

How could they think such a thing? "No, they didn't. Surely. Eleanor was a married woman, Georgie." Had his private meetings with Eleanor become public knowledge? They were entirely innocent— just two old friends sharing tea and conversation. But the ton would not believe that.

Georgie shook her head. "Married to a man who had been incarcerated with syphillic lunacy. People knew the old story, and they saw how well the pair of you got on. No one was willing to challenge the power of the Duchess of Haverford by making a play for you."

Ruth nodded. "But then she came back to Town late last year

and the two of you avoided one another or were distantly polite. Of course, all the female sharks started circling."

"I don't understand why you are still at odds," Cherry said. "Aunt Eleanor was wrong, of course. She should have spoken to us about her concerns and left us to make our own decision. But no harm was done in the end, and she has apologised."

"It was the manner of it," James explained. "She went behind her son's back and spoke to you in secret, and tried to use that dreadful event from your past to force you to her way of thinking. It was cruel, manipulative and deceitful. She is not the woman I thought her."

"Then perhaps," Georgie suggested, "It is your view of her at fault. You idealised her, and now you demonise her."

"Steady on, Georgie," James protested. "That's a little harsh."

"Is it?" Georgie looked around at the other women, and must have been encouraged by what she saw in their eyes, for she continued. "I do not condone Eleanor's interference between Cherry and her son, but every person in this room has benefited from what you call her manipulation and deceit in her management of our personal scandals. You have called on her yourself, James, to bury inconvenient truths and promote the version of whatever story we have chosen to present to Society."

James shook his head. "That is quite a different thing."

"Not entirely," Ruth argued. "Unless you are saying you are comfortable with her using her skills to manipulate the ton on behalf of family and friends, but not on family and friends. I suppose I can see your point."

Georgie had not finished. "You do not understand her, James. She is not a perfect woman. But nor are any of us. She *is* a strong and caring one. Powerful, too. Do you realise what an incredible thing that is? She was married against her will to a brutal tyrant who tried to control every aspect of her life. I have seen so many women turn into pale shadows of themselves under those circumstances. My own sister-in-law, for one."

She turned to Cherry. "One of the best things to happen to your mother was being taken under Eleanor's wing. Eleanor shared with

Grace—and with me, too—the skills she had painfully taught herself. How to use our positions as a wife and a daughter of powerful men to build a network of personal power that the men who ruled us had to respect. How to go behind their backs when deceit was the only way to look after those we loved. How to gather information about those with power over us to use against them when our freedom or our safety was at risk."

She glared at James, her eyes burning. "If you have never experienced what she has, James, then you have no right to judge her. Find her actions wrong, if they are. But do not decide that she is not worthy of your respect. There is no finer friend a woman like me could have. Cherry, too, should be grateful Eleanor became the lady that she is, for all the sweetness in Haverford's character would have been destroyed long since by his father without his mother's desperate battle for influence over his upbringing."

"I am grateful," Cherry agreed. "Anthony and I know all too well what we owe to her."

James felt the ground on which his anger rest melt beneath him. He had once been a prisoner, and then a slave, in far off Iran, which the English call Persia. And in those days, he had lied and stolen in order to eat. He had flattered his captor with false words to win a modicum of freedom. And he had never counted his deceit against his honour.

"She was still wrong to go behind her son's back," he grumbled.

His ladies heard the unspoken surrender in his remark, and smiled at one another.

کمبل همه چیز برای عشق

Eleanor, Cherry, and Jessica came out of the fabric emporium to find a row of coaches lined along their side of the street. A large family had arrived in several coaches, and their coachmen were taking it in turns to disgorge the occupants.

They could see the Haverford carriage, pulled in to the other side, some thirty paces away where the street widened.

Eleanor suggested waiting until the queue of coaches had

offloaded their passengers and moved away, though who knew how long that would take. The one currently in front of the door had been there for more than five minutes while seven young ladies disembarked, and several then climbed aboard again, only to re-emerge, waving something triumphantly—a shawl, a reticule, a handkerchief.

"One wonders where they all sat," Cherry whispered to Jessica. "Look, that is the fourth lady to return to the coach because she has forgotten something. Let us walk, Aunt Eleanor. It is only a matter of yards."

"Perhaps thirty yards, and on the other side of the road," Eleanor pointed out. "Furthermore, both path and road are patched with ice."

"We shall be careful," Cherry promised, and led the way down the two steps from the shop. Jessica was close behind her, but several ladies from the coach chose that moment to squeeze through the door. Eleanor and her footman were forced to wait.

By the time they descended to the path, Cherry and Jessica were just disappearing behind the coach directly outside and the heads of the next coach's lead horses.

"Hurry ahead to escort the young ladies," Eleanor told the foot-man. "Take care on the ice."

She took care herself, slowly placing her feet and moving her weight so that this shopping expedition did not end in a nasty fall. Cherry and Jessica had not got far ahead. She could hear them just beyond the coach, talking about their purchases as they waited for a gap in the traffic that streamed down this busy street.

Eleanor rounded the back of the coach, stepping off the paved path. Yes, there they were. She sent up a silent prayer of thanks that her maid had insisted on her wearing pattens. They held her up above the worst of the noxious mess of ice, gravel, mud and horse manure that successive hooves had stirred to a slurry.

The first she knew of the impending tragedy was the jingle of harness and the dull splash of hooves in the mud, too fast for the narrow space. After that, events unfolded so quickly that it was only in successive nightmares she understood the sequence. A man dashed past her, under the horses heads, hands outstretched. The Haverford footman grabbed at him, but slipped on a patch of ice so he fell. Not before he had grasped a handful of the man's jacket, but it was not enough and too late to stop those hands from shoving Cherry straight into the forequarters of the near horse of the pair that had just trotted into Eleanor's view. The man wrenched his jacket loose and took off down the street.

Jessica had hold of Cherry's redingote and was pulling her back, out from under the hooves and the perilous wheel of the curricle that sped behind. The horse lashed out with its hind hoof just as Cherry fell back, landing on top of Jessica.

Eleanor had no idea how she crossed the distance—and the recumbent footman. She found herself kneeling beside Cherry and Jessica, begging them to tell her they were all right. Jessica had had the breath knocked out of her, but she nodded. Cherry was nearly as white as the snow that chose that moment to begin falling, soft heavy flakes, wafting gently to land on Cherry's gloved hands, held to her abdomen one each side of the dirty mark—the dirty horse-shoe-shaped mark—on her redingote.

A crowd quickly gathered. The footman. The driver of the curricle, stammering apologies. The Haverford coachman. Several members of the family whose awkward parking had laid the foundations for this disaster. Other passers-by. All chattering like an evening chorus of starlings as they offered advice, asked questions, and laid blame.

Eleanor ignored most of them, taking Cherry's hand and squeezing it. "Do not try to move, Cherry. William." William was the footman. "Find a board wide enough for us to move the duchess lying flat. Harris?" Harris was the coachman. "Is this one of the carriages that converts to a bed? If so, convert it."

Cherry managed a tremulous smile. "I must be squashing Jessica."

"You will keep still, my dear," Eleanor insisted. "The horse caught her with its hind hoof, Jessica. We will not allow her to move on her own until she has been examined by a doctor." She turned to look at the driver of the curricle, who was still wittering on about how sorry he was. She had a vague notion that she had seen him before on the outskirts of some of the lesser social events. He was barely old enough to shave, and thin in the way of a boy just coming out of a growth spurt. Otherwise, the most notable things about him were his wide frightened eyes and his blindingly yellow waistcoat.

"Young man, you may put your regret and your equipage to good use by going to the Earl of Ashbury's house, on Beecham Square. If the Countess of Ashbury is at home, tell her there has been an accident and the Duchess of Haverford needs her. She will find us…" Eleanor thought of the distance to Haverford House. No that would not do. "She will find us at Winshire House in Lambton Square."

"Yes, Ma'am. But should I not fetch a doctor?"

"Lady Ashbury is a doctor, and a very good one. If she is not at home, her household staff will tell you where to find her. I am trusting you to bring her to the duchess's aid."

The boy gulped, but nodded. "I will, Ma'am." He turned miserable eyes to Cherry. "I am so sorry, Your Grace." He heaved himself into his curricle and set the fidgety team off at a trot even faster than the one that had caused the trouble.

Eleanor raised her voice to address the coachman for the team that shifted restlessly less than a yard from where Jessica and Cherry lay. He gawked at them from his perch, the reins slack in his hands. "You there! Move your coach back to give us some room. And someone instruct the other coachman to move his forward." One of the fashionable gentlemen gawking from the crowd touched his top hat. "Yes, Ma'am. Immediately. Smith! Do what the lady says!" He took off up the side of the other coach.

William returned carrying one end of a board which he had covered with a shawl, the other end supported by one of the warehouse men from the fabric emporium. Eleanor supervised the careful transfer of Cherry from her position half on the road and half on Jessica onto the board.

"Do not try to help, Cherry. Let us do all the work," she scolded.

She dragooned two men from among the onlookers to help

carry the board to the Haverford carriage, taking extreme care over the icy road. The coachman had converted the seats into a bed that took up the whole space, and they passed the board inside until it was resting across the bed, with one end out each door. Again, they carefully moved Cherry, and then Jessica and Eleanor settled on the bed, one each side of Cherry, holding her hands.

"I hurt, Aunt Eleanor," Cherry admitted. She gripped Eleanor's hand, tears standing in her eyes. "I am afraid for the baby."

"I have sent for Ruth," Eleanor reminded her. "She will know what to do, my darling."

The Haverford coachman kept his horses to a slow walk, avoiding all the ruts and hollows that he could. William walked ahead and another co-opted volunteer from the crowd behind to warn the traffic that the coach carried an injured person, and would not be hurried. When they arrived at the Winshire townhouse some ten minutes later, Ruth was already there.

7

James was watching Haverford exercise a blend of charm, persuasion, and ruthless focus on his personal goals to bring the other members of this committee of Lords to the conclusion that James and Haverford had long since reached. He had a way of discovering their motivations and personal interests, and using those to convince the recalcitrants that providing shelter against the winter cold to homeless soldiers and their families would not undermine the well-being of the British Empire.

With the thorough verbal beating James had taken from his womenfolk still much on his mind, he realised the political skills he had always admired in the young duke, Haverford had learned from his mother.

The uncomfortable train of thought was interrupted when a pair of his Para Daisian retainers burst into the room, over the protests of the parliamentary footman who was trying to deny them entry. "Prince," one of them called out in Farsi, as the footman was reinforced by a couple of burly comrades.

James stood. "Let them through," he insisted. "They have a message for me."

The footmen reluctantly separated, and the two Para Daisians hurried down the room to where he stood. The spokesman started to speak, caught himself back, and began again in English. "Your Grace, you must come. You and the Duke of Haverford. There has been an accident." He turned to look at Haverford. "It is your wife, bey. Lady Ashbury said to tell you she is aware and talking, but you must come."

Haverford was already on his feet and moving towards the coats and hats that were on the table near the door. James inclined his head to the other committee members. "You must excuse us, gentlemen."

They indicated their agreement, but James had not waited for it.

"We have horses, your graces, in the Old Palace Yard," one of the retainers said, and Haverford turned through a door to lead the way down several flights of narrow stairs James hadn't seen before. Another door let on to a corridor outside of the House of Lords, and the small group hurried around several more corners before passing the guards on the Peers' Door from the Old Palace Yard.

Haverford paused as he accepted the horse that third retainer led to him. "Lady Ashbury is with her, you said?"

The retainer confirmed it, and added, "Your Grace's mother had her brought to Winshire House, because it was closer."

Haverford nodded, mounted, and touched his heels to the horse, which leapt forward and cantered past the guards on the gate into St Margaret's Street and up the street on his way to Mayfair. He had the unfamiliar horse, and one of the independent fiery Turkmen stallions at that, under full control as he pushed the pace almost, but not quite, beyond the point the traffic allowed. James and his men kept up, but did not try to deny him the lead.

It still took ten minutes before they pulled up before the Winshire townhouse. Haverford and James tossed their reins to the retainers and leapt the few steps to the front door, which opened as they approached to allow them immediate access into the house.

James ignored the skinny youth in a flashy waistcoat sitting huddled and miserable on one side of the steps. His men would deal with it.

Inside, his son-in-law, Ruth's husband Val, was just coming

down the stairs with Haverford's sister Jessica. She had been crying. When she saw her brother, she pulled her hand from Val's arm and threw herself down the last few steps and into her brother's arms.

"I tried to keep her from falling, Anthony," she insisted. "If only we'd waited like Aunt Eleanor wanted!"

James looked past the brother and sister to Val, raising an interrogative eyebrow.

"Ruth and Aunt Eleanor are with her," he said. "Haverford, you are to go up."

Haverford pulled away from his sister and set off up the stairs, but Val caught his arm to stop him. "Ruth thinks Cherry is not much more than bruised, but Haverford? She took a horse's hoof to the abdomen. Not full strength, thank God. She was falling backwards at the time. But Ruth is concerned about the baby."

It was the first James knew about Cherry's pregnancy. He clasped Haverford's shoulder in silent sympathy.

Haverford's already drawn face paled even more, but he gave Val a jerky nod of acknowledgement and continued up the stairs.

Waiting was hard. Ruth would allow only Eleanor, Haverford, and Cherry's dresser into the bedchamber where Cherry rested. The servant had invited herself, dragooning the groom to drive her from Haverford House as soon as she heard that her mistress had been in an accident.

From time to time one of those in attendance would take a brief break to attend their personal needs, and to update those who waited with any changes in Cherry's condition.

At first, Ruth was cautiously optimistic. There was bruising, she said, but no bleeding and no contractions.

After hearing what Jessica had to say about the fall, James set himself the task of finding the assailant. He sent for the boy huddled on the steps, the Haverford footman William, and the private enquiry agents, the Wakefields. He deputed his friend and aid, Yousef, to organise Winshire servants to canvass the scene, looking for witnesses. He questioned William and the youth, who introduced himself as Paul Mandeville and was indeed the driver of the curricle, and consumed with guilt.

James didn't mince his words. "You did not push the duchess, Mr Mandeville. The blame for her fall goes to the man who did. You were, by all accounts, driving too fast, and can bear the burden of knowing that you offered a villain his opportunity to do harm. You can make amends by telling me everything you observed."

Mandeville was little help. He had seen a shape in a coat and hat, hurrying away. His description added to what Jessica could remember only gave a general approximation of height and an indication of spry movement that possibly suggested a young man. The figure was bundled up against the cold in a long coat, a scarf, and a cap pulled down over the eyes, so that neither witness could swear even it was a man or a woman.

Then the butler announced David Wakefield, principal of the enquiry firm and incidentally half-brother to the current Duke of Haverford. David listened to James's terse recital of the facts and had a few more questions for Jessica and Mandeville.

After Wakefield left, taking Mandeville with him, Frances Grenford arrived with her governess, and Jessica took her up to see Rosemary and the Winderfield schoolroom party. James tried to work at his desk for a while, but his mind wouldn't settle as he worried about Cherry.

Haverford, when he popped in briefly to see James after a trip to the necessary, approved the measures James had taken. "I want him caught, and I want to know why she was pushed and who he is working for," he said. "It is good to know I can leave it to you while I focus on Cherry."

"How is she?" James asked.

"There is some bleeding. Ruth says all we can do is wait. I cannot lose her, Winshire." The last was an anguished cry. "I must get back to her. Excuse me."

Jessica entered the room as Haverford was leaving it, and threw herself on her brother's chest, babbling apologies for failing to save his wife. "As I heard it," Haverford told her, "you stopped her from going under the wheels. I am so grateful, Jessica. She might have died if you had not grabbed for her."

Jessica lifted a tear-stained face. "Truly?"

"Truly," Haverford insisted. "Jessie, I am going to send Mama downstairs. Try to get her to eat something, will you?"

James called for a footman and sent him to the kitchens with an order for food—something appetising that would slip down easily. Tea, too. They had Eleanor's preferred pekoe. Though she might want something more bracing this afternoon.

As if they sensed the advent of food and potential news, Rosemary and Drew appeared just before the dowager duchess and the refreshments arrived together. Eleanor let Jessica fuss over her, filling a plate with little tarts and savouries, pouring her tea just the way she liked it. Watching, James realised what Eleanor was doing. Jessica needed to be of service. Not being allowed to help with the care of Cherry left her feeling raw and useless.

James counted himself good with people, and he'd known that Jessica was upset and shaken. But Eleanor had immediately understood why, and had done what she could do to help. It made it all the more mysterious that she so badly underestimated her own son and his feelings for Cherry.

She realises it, Grace said. She must feel terrible. Especially now this has happened.

He offered an olive branch. "Eleanor, I would like to have rooms made up for you and your wards, if it pleases you. Cherry will want you to stay near, I imagine. And Jessica and Frances will worry if they are not close."

She accepted the overture. "Thank you, James. That is very kind of you."

"Make a list of what you will need," he suggested, "and I will send someone to fetch it."

"I will go, Aunt Eleanor," Jessica offered. "I can make a list of what Frances and I need, and supervise it being packed. Frances stayed in the schoolroom. She will be fine without me for a short time."

"I shall keep an eye on Frances, Your Grace," Rosemary offered.

Eleanor put a hand briefly on her ward's. "Thank you, Jessica dearest. It would be a tremendous help. And thank you, Lady Rosemary."

"I shall escort you, Miss Grenford, if I may," Drew said.

James fetched paper and a pencil and handed them to Jessica, who took a list to Eleanor's dictation while Drew arranged a carriage. "Her brother's wife was attacked today. Guard her with that in mind," James told Drew.

Jessica left, Rosemary went upstairs to join the schoolroom party, and Eleanor returned to the room where Cherry waited to find out the consequences of her injuries.

James was left alone, frustrated by his inability to do anything to help his niece beyond ordering other people to drive carriages, make beds, and hunt down miscreants. He wished that Eleanor had thought to find him a task.

8

───────

The trickle of blood became a flow as the afternoon wore on. Once contractions started, Eleanor knew the chance of saving Cherry's precious burden had been lost. The battle to keep Cherry alive continued throughout the evening and into the night.

Anthony would not leave his wife's side. Nor did Cherry want him to go. Even before her condition deteriorated, when they were just waiting and hoping for the best, she followed him with her eyes each time he left the room, slumped into melancholy while he was gone, and reached out a hand to draw him nearer as soon as he stepped back inside the door. During her travail, she said, his strength bolstered hers.

Even so, she was weakening, and the calm confidence she had worn as a mask earlier in the day had fragmented and disappeared. "You will not leave me?" she asked Anthony, periodically. He had sat for hours beside her, holding her hand. Each time, he replied, "Never, my love. How could I leave my heart?"

To Eleanor's surprise, both Cherry and Anthony begged her to stay, too. Eleanor did not believe she had much to offer, but if it gave her son and his wife comfort to have her there, she would stay, holding Cherry's other hand when the contractions strengthened,

188

wringing water out of cloths and bathing her face, spooning sips of water into her mouth when it became dry.

There was a time when the fight became desperate. The poor little mite had finally been expelled from its haven, and the afterbirth with it. For a few frantic minutes, blood gushed. Ruth and Cherry's dresser worked frantically doing things that Eleanor could not watch. Eleanor clutched Cherry's hand, praying more fervently than she ever had in her life. Anthony begged Cherry over and over, "Breathe, my love. Keep breathing. Stay with me, Cherry. We have so much love still to live. Don't leave me."

At last, Ruth stood back, heaved a sigh, and gave Anthony a tenuous smile. "She is still with us, Haverford. Please God, we can keep her. She will be weak, but the worst of the bleeding has stopped. Now, all we have to do is avoid fever."

Ruth sent Cherry's dresser off to bed, pointing out that she would be needed in the next week and should be fresh for whatever her mistress required. Ruth herself washed behind the dressing screen, and returned. "Perhaps you should go to bed, too, duchess. If there are no changes in the next hour, I will get some rest myself, and so should you, Haverford."

"I will sleep here," Anthony declared. He put his head on the bed next to his wife, and within minutes was fast asleep, still holding her hand.

"I will stay with you," Eleanor decided. Ruth looked as tired and drawn as Anthony, and needed someone to talk to or she, too, would fall asleep on a chair. Eleanor asked a few questions about what changes to look for, and then she and Ruth talked quietly about the family members they had in common through the marriage between Cherry and Anthony.

Anthony and Cherry slept on.

When the clock struck the hour—three bongs—Ruth yawned and stood. "Go to bed, Your Grace. Get some sleep. Please send someone to sit with these two, and I will go to bed myself."

Eleanor found a footman in the hall, waiting to take messages. She told him to find someone to replace Lady Asbury, and he said

Lady Rosemary had asked to be fetched. He set off to knock on the lady's door.

When he was out of sight, Eleanor realised that she had no idea which bedchamber she had been assigned. She set off for the guest wing on the other side of the stairwell, hoping a footman might be awake there to direct her. But as she crossed the upper landing, she saw light spilling from a doorway downstairs. Someone was in the drawing room.

Perhaps it was Rosemary. Eleanor should check, and if so, send her up to Ruth.

But when she entered the room, she found James sitting, staring into the embers, deep in thought. He must've heard her in the doorway, for he turned, stood, and took a step towards her. Whatever he saw on her face, he held out his arms and Eleanor ran into them and burst into tears.

کمبل همه چیز برای عشق

James had no idea what kind of nonsense he spouted as he held Eleanor tenderly, supporting her weight with his arms around her, patting her back, letting the long hours of iron control loose in an abandonment of grief.

He had heard the reports, how she had taken charge at the scene of the accident. She did everything that needed to be done, except, perhaps, she could have thought to send someone after the assailant. All the reports he had received so far said the same thing —no one had a single clue that led anywhere. They had a vague description and a coat with empty pockets. And nothing more.

He was thinking as a military commander. Eleanor's focus was on Cherry, as it should have been—on getting her help as quickly as possible. Then she spent fifteen hours supporting Cherry and Haverford through their ordeal—always calm, always encouraging, Ruth had said when he had met her on her way to bed.

The respect she had won from him since his return to England four years ago, that he thought lost, had returned full force.

Eventually, the stormy tears settled to a quieter weeping. He coaxed her to the chair by the fire and sat, settling her on his knee. He wiped her eyes with his handkerchief. She rested against him, totally spent, occasionally hiccupping another sob. "I have made your shoulder all wet," she murmured.

"Not for the first time," James assured her. "I have four daughters, remember." Although it had been years since his had been their favoured shoulder when life was too cruel to bear. He had not held a woman in his arms for a long time, and this one was not his daughter. Tired as he was, his body reminded him that he desired her.

He shifted her slightly away from the evidence of his inappropriate response. "Would you like a port or a brandy? Something to help you sleep?"

She chuckled. "I will sleep as soon as my head hits the pillow. But I don't know which room my things are in. I saw the light and came to see if it was someone who could direct me." She reached and cupped his face with her hand, and he had to exert an iron control not to turn his mouth into her palm and kiss it. He would not seduce her while she was so emotionally raw.

And his mind raced on to a future time, when she was not so vulnerable. For he would seduce her. Yes, and marry her, too, if she would have him.

She was speaking again, and he must pay attention. "I did not intend to weep all over you. I apologise, James."

"It was my privilege. You have carried your family today; I am proud to be the person you did not have to be strong for. I think, perhaps, you do not realise how amazing you are, for it is what you always do. It is I who should apologise to you, for my cruel words and my coldness after your mistake with Cherry and your son. I hope you will forgive me for being such a self-righteous idiot. My female relatives have pointed out that I am not so perfect myself that I have a right to demand perfection from my friends. Can we be friends again, Eleanor? Will you forgive me?"

The tears welled again but she smiled as she dashed at them with his handkerchief. "I am not usually such a watering pot," she complained. "James, if you can forgive me, I can forgive you.

Though I was the one in the wrong. Cherry and Anthony belong together. You should have seen them, James, each being strong for the other. And then, when Cherry seemed to be slipping away from us, Anthony's desperation…" She turned her welling eyes into his shoulder again, but only for a moment before she had blinked back the tears and lifted her wonderful eyes up to his.

"Friends again," she said.

And sweethearts, he wanted to say, but this was not the time. Instead, he asked again about a drink.

Eleanor uncurled from his lap, and rose to her feet. "If I may, I will take it up to bed with me. If you will tell me where my bed is?"

"I will show you upstairs," James promised. "I am off to bed myself."

And he ignored all the naughty suggestions from his suddenly riotous body, and showed her to her room, leaving her at her door like a gentleman ought.

9

Physically, Cherry recovered quickly. Two days after the incident, Anthony moved them all—Cherry, Eleanor, and his two half-sisters—back to Haverford House. Eleanor was sorry to go. She had slept most of the day after her reconciliation with James. Who knew what might have come from meeting him casually in the course of the day while living in his house?

Her primary duty was to her family, and Cherry wanted to be home.

February drifted into March. Anthony took Cherry away to the little estate he owned in Sussex on the coast. Frances and her friend Daisy went with them to keep Cherry company when Anthony had to come up for a vote on the Lords. And Frances's governess, too, to make sure that the girls were kept productively busy when Anthony and Cherry wanted time on their own.

That left Eleanor and Jessica to prepare for Jessica's long-delayed wedding, which was fast approaching. Eleanor was also busy with the many philanthropic ventures she had volunteered her time for late last year.

When she received a letter from a distant Grenford connection, seeking her help, she was delighted to discover that the young lady had heard she sometime took a secretary, and was applying for the position.

It was a sad story. The girl's uncle had invested his entire fortune in several trading opportunities, lost heavily, and shot himself rather than face his creditors. Marigold Grenford-Smith had been left destitute, and was about to be turned out onto the street.

Eleanor sent for Marigold immediately, as well as researching her name in the family tree. If the girl turned out to be what she claimed, Eleanor would hire her. Even if she was exaggerating the relationship, she might still be of assistance to Eleanor. In any case, Eleanor would surely be able to find a position for her somewhere.

But there it was. A cousin eight or nine times removed had married a Mr Smith and their son had taken the double name, perhaps in the hope that some lustre from his distant relatives might reflect onto him. Sadly, he and his wife had died leaving a six-year-old daughter, Marigold, who had been raised by her mother's brother.

The interview was a success, and Marigold moved into Haverford House, where she soon showed herself competent to take over all of Eleanor's list-checking and much of her lesser correspondence.

Fortunately. For Eleanor now had to make time each week to meet with James at Miss Clemens' Emporium. He was always the perfect gentleman. It was very disappointing.

They fell back into the way of comparing their diaries and meeting at various entertainments. James thanked Eleanor for keeping the vultures at bay. She just wished that the many ladies who acknowledged her prior right to his time were correct about his interest.

Eleanor knew that under the right circumstances he could desire her physically. On the night she had lost all sense of decorum and thrown herself on him in floods of tears, she had felt his physical reaction. When he did nothing about it, she knew it was just the male body responding to an apparently available female one, plastered across his body. James was far too much the gentleman to act on his lust when his feelings were not involved.

Friends, he said. She would have to be satisfied with that.

She did her best to behave as if she had not felt the same physical tug—that her feelings for him were the same kind of affection towards a brother that she felt for Henry Redepenning or Tolly.

Hope was not quite extinguished, however. She waited for a sign from him that a deeper connection would be appreciated. It never came.

The investigation never did uncover the assailant. Anthony was certain he was still out there. Anthony's favourite horse nearly died after someone introduced dried ragwort into its hay. Someone shot at Jessica while she and Colyton took an early morning ride in Hyde Park.

A Haverford carriage that had carried the ladies to a ball was sabotaged. After the driver went missing, James insisted on a detailed inspection and found a damaged axle. He sent Eleanor and Jessica home in a Winshire carriage, with one of his own men to drive and several others as escorts. The driver was found later that day—tied up in a nearby mews, with a thundering headache from a blow to the head.

There were several other incidents, and perhaps some of them were truly accidents. Still, Anthony added several Bow Street Runners and half a dozen ex-soldiers to his immediate staff, and begged his mother and sisters to go nowhere without their escort. When Cherry's sister Sarah came up to town in late March with her son, her young step-sisters, and her new baby, Cherry returned from the seaside. Anthony doubled the guard.

By the middle of April, when nothing had happened for four weeks, the danger appeared to be over, but Anthony continued to insist on them taking careful precautions.

"Mama," Anthony said at a dinner one evening, "Cherry and I have been discussing a trip to visit Jonathan. The weather should be good for travelling in May, after Jessica's wedding. Would you like to come?"

It was hugely tempting. Eleanor vacillated for several days, wondering who she could get to take over her commitments in England, daydreaming about seeing her darling Jonathan and meeting his new wife and children, contemplating another long stretch of time estranged from James—this time by distance. They would be gone at least six months, and perhaps up to a year.

In the end, she suggested that Anthony and Cherry go without her. "Perhaps I shall make the trip next year. I could take Frances, and you could hire me a courier to assure my safe passage."

All her thinking had made one thing clear. She did not want to keep waiting for James. Once the wedding was over and Society had retreated from London, she was going to put their friendship to the test by telling him how she felt.

She told no one her full plan. They knew she planned to retreat to the country after Cherry and Haverford departed, and that Frances was going to spend the summer in the North with her friend Sarah Overton.

Eleanor was looking forward to a peaceful few weeks at Holly-stone Hall before visiting with friends. Only Marigold knew that she was not going directly to Hollystone Hall, but had taken a town-house at Leamington Priors. She told Marigold, who made the arrangements for her, that she intended to take the waters. She hoped that, visiting a lesser spa town at an unfashionable time of the year, she might go unnoticed. "To this end, dear Marigold, I shall take only my dresser, the coachman, and a single groom. You shall go on to Hollystone Hall and have a little holiday.

Before she left, she would send James a letter inviting him to join her. And then they would see what they would see.

Colyton's mother and Colyton's three daughters arrived in London several days before the wedding. Lady Colyton had been living retired in the country for some years and had never moved in the same circles as Eleanor, so a dinner Cherry hosted was the first opportunity that Jessica's family had to meet the lady.

"Perhaps she was over-awed by her company," Cherry said, charitably, the following morning.

"Yes, perhaps." Eleanor voiced the agreement, but privately thought that Lady Colyton thought herself too good for the company. The brief and rare comments she had made were all animadversions about the morals of the fashionable world.

Jessica had no concerns. "I am not marrying Colyton's mother, Aunt Eleanor." She shrugged. "Colyton says she will be moving to a townhouse in Cheltenham as soon as we are wed. I will be there to supervise the children and the servants, so she will no longer be needed."

If Colyton's mother was less than happy about the marriage, his daughters were ecstatic. Eleanor had asked to meet them, and Colyton brought them for afternoon tea with Eleanor, Cherry, Jessica, and her sisters. The three little girls were polite, but very quiet. However, when Jessica asked if they would be her attendants at the wedding, along with Frances, the youngest girl pounced on her heels with glee. The eldest cast an anxious glance at their father. The middle child piped up, "Grandmere says that children do not go to weddings. Children should not be heard, and preferably not seen."

Jessica met Colyford's eyes as she said, "I am sure your grandmother will agree that on her wedding day a bride has a right to decide who comes to the wedding. Unless your father forbids it," and an incipient glare hinted that he would be in for an argument if he tried, "you shall come to my wedding."

Colyton frowned.

Eleanor could not resist. "Perhaps Lady Colyton, living retired as she does, does not realise that the rules are different for close relatives of the bride and groom. When the Earl and Countess of Ashbury married, his daughters were her attendants, and at the time, they were younger than any of you."

"Yes, and my nephew was at my wedding," Cherry said.

Colyton inclined his head. "How can I refuse my bride? I shall speak with Mother."

And so, when the day came, three very excited little girls stood with Frances, all of them dressed in shades of pink with coronets of flowers. Their grandmother need have no qualms about their manners. Despite nearly bursting with excitement, they all behaved beautifully. Afterwards, Eleanor complimented them, but she noticed the dowager Lady Colyton found cause to correct each one for a miniscule fault, and had nothing nice to say to any of them.

Colyton had put on a breakfast at his townhouse, organised by Jessica with the help of Marigold. When Eleanor arrived at the house, she saw the dowager Lady Colyton climbing into a coach full of baggage. She was, Eleanor found, already leaving for Cheltenham.

The following day, Colyton and the new Lady Colyton took the girls home to his estate in Oxfordshire, and a week later it was time to say goodbye to Cherry and Haverford, and then Frances and the Overtons.

Finally, Eleanor also left London, on her own great adventure, in her reticule a brief note in response to her letter to James. "Yes. I will be there by Tuesday evening." It was signed, simply, "J".

10

All went well with Eleanor's plan until they stopped in Tring for lunch. From there, she would lose the other coaches in the procession that the old duke had always insisted was due to her station. They would continue on to Hollyford Hall. She and her three trusted servants would progress to Leamington.

But when it was time to board the coach, Fletcher, her dresser, was in agony with stomach cramps. Eleanor sent for a doctor, who administered a purge. "She will do now," he said at last. "But she must stay in bed for at least the next two days." He thought it must be something she ate, and Fletcher admitted to a double helping of mushrooms. Nobody else was ill, but one bad mushroom might have made its way into her serving by mistake.

Marigold, bless her, said that she would stay and care for Fletcher, and conduct her on to Hollystone Hall when she was well enough to be moved. "That would mean you have to hire a local girl to be your maid," she added, doubtfully.

Fletcher tried to sit up at that, which set off another round of retching. When she could, she said to Eleanor, "You take Miss Grenford, Your Grace. I will do very well with Mary." Mary was Fletcher's assistant, and also her niece.

Eleanor supposed she could take Mary, but that would mean letting someone else into her secret. Marigold had rented the townhouse for her under her chosen pseudonym, so knew where she was going and what the servants hired with the house thought she was called.

Marigold did not know that Eleanor was hoping that James would join her, but time enough to tell the girl that when James made his decision.

I don't like to leave Fletcher while she is so sick. Besides, it is too late to leave now. Her heart quailed at the thought of missing her opportunity, and having to go through all this subterfuge again, but then she brightened. *If Fletcher is better in the morning, I can leave early. I can make the trip in one day rather than spend the night in Bodicote, as I had planned. I will still be there when James arrives.*

"I'll do that if you are better by morning," Eleanor agreed.

کمبل همه چیز برای عشق

James rode into the town of Leamington Priors late on Monday evening. The sun had set an hour ago, and he'd ridden the last few miles by starlight, giving thanks for his horse's superior night vision and hearing, and the clear starlit sky. Tuesday, Eleanor had said, but he did not want to be late, so instead, he was early.

He wondered what she had in mind. He had spent the last two months watching for some sign that she would welcome his courtship. Nothing until the letter. Two months of civil distance and then an invitation to meet him in private. In a town where they might reasonably expect to be anonymous.

If it was anyone else, he would assume she was seeking an affair. Even though it was Eleanor, that pattern card of virtue, he could not imagine any other reason for the secrecy and the secluded location. The idea both attracted and repelled him. He wanted her—of course he did. For the rest of their lives, not just for a few nights hidden away out of sight of their families and the world.

He decided to ride past the address she had given him. It was on a small square down a quiet side street. Just an anonymous townhouse in a row of townhouses. It crossed his mind that tomorrow night he might be invited to stay. With Eleanor, in her bed. He forgave himself the fantasy. He was, after all, only a man.

Perhaps he should call tonight!

But it was late, and only two of the windows showed lights—a dim one flickering through the glass panel to the side of the front door, and brighter illumination behind a window higher up the building—probably a servant's room in the attic.

As he watched, a man walked up to the front door. Before he could knock, it opened, and he stepped inside. A footman? Someone who belonged, in any case, since Eleanor's servants had been watching for the man and had let him in without hesitation.

Perhaps James should stop by, and check that all was well. As he tried to tell himself the thought was not thoroughly self-serving, the lights in the attic were quenched. That was it, then. The household had gone to bed. James would leave Eleanor to sleep and see her in the morning.

کمبل همه چیز برای عشق

Nine o'clock in the morning was far too early to call on a lady. James was being ridiculous. He had climbed the fence into the small garden in the centre of the square, and was sitting on a bench in the middle of the space, peering through the bushes to see the first sign of movement at Eleanor's house.

The flowers he had purchased on his ride through town this morning would be thoroughly wilted before any reasonable upper-class household was awake. Unless Eleanor was as anxious as he, and up early, he would have to throw them away and pick another bunch from the garden around him.

He should whistle for his horse, the Turkmen stallion Xander. They had gone for an early morning ride to shake out the fidgets and ended up here. He should go back to his inn, have breakfast, and return at a reasonable hour. He could not bring himself to leave.

Duke arrested for loitering in square and stealing flowers. Wouldn't that be a headline for *The Teatime Tattler*. *Found guilty of being hopelessly besotted.* His hope had swung the full pendulum back to believing that, even if her intention was a brief affair, he could persuade her to matrimony.

Yes, she had had a bad experience of the wedded state, but he would promise her all the independence she needed to feel safe, sign anything she cared to put before him so her property remained in her own hands, do anything she needed to be convinced that his heart was hers.

And if she demurred at first? He would let her seduce him, of course. It was the gentlemanly thing to do.

کمبل همه چیز برای عشق

"How could you, Marigold?" Eleanor asked her former secretary. Not that she had fired the treacherous female, but conspiring with a criminal to disable her servants and abduct Eleanor herself was surely tantamount to a resignation.

"I am merely seeking a better position, Your Grace," Marigold sneered. "One your money will buy me."

"Us," said her collaborator. "You will buy us a future, Ellie. Do your friends call you Ellie? Your son took everything I have and you owe me. My first idea was to kill you, Haverford's wife, and all three of his sisters. Let him feel what I felt when he took everything away from me."

He slipped his arms around Marigold from behind and fondled both her breasts. She tipped her head back, and he bent to kiss and then lick her neck, which made the girl groan.

Marigold surrendered utterly to the sensual spell the boy wove, but he was watching Eleanor the whole time, his eyes cold and alert.

She gave no reaction—to his words, or to his behaviour.

One of his hands crept down Marigold's body to the cleft between her legs. Eleanor steeled herself to show nothing.

Marigold's words stopped his hand. "But you have me, now, Kit. And when we get our money, we will be able to run far away. We will have everything, you and I."

Kit nuzzled her neck again, before letting her go. "Everything," he said. "Including my revenge. You should be grateful, Your Grace. Marigold's idea was much better than mine. Have you written the letter, darling?"

Marigold nodded. "Ten thousand pounds, in gold. It will take them a while to get that much, Kit. Could we not settle for less?"

He rounded on his accomplice, snarling. "I am already settling! They owe me their lives!" He took a deep breath and let it out slowly then visibly forced a conciliatory smile. "We will give them time, darling. I have it all planned. You have done a wonderful job, and no one will know where we have gone."

He turned his attention back to Eleanor, his smile gone. "Now. I can untie you, and you can walk out of here yourself, keeping your mouth shut, and climbing into the carriage like a good little dowager duchess. I will have a gun and a knife on you at all times. I warn you not to make any fuss! I really did like my first plan."

He sighed. "But I have promised Marigold not to hurt you as long as you behave, so if you cannot give me your solemn promise that you will not attempt to escape or to attract attention, I will just have to knock you out, gag you, and take you out the back door rolled up in a sheet." His smile was stretching of the teeth without an iota of humour.

Eleanor chose to walk under her own control, down the servant stairs and out of the kitchen door. She should have suspected something last night, when they arrived to an empty house. Marigold said there must be a mistake, and she would sort it out in the morning. Instead, she, her treacherous secretary, and the girl's lover were the only people in the house.

What of her coachman and guard, who should be in the mews on the other side of the lane? But there was no sign of them. Outside, the only signs of life were the pair of horses hitched to a plain dark carriage.

If only she had arranged for James to come first thing this morning! But surely, when he discovered her gone, he would investigate? Eleanor had no idea how her servants had been disabled, but if James found them, he would know that something was wrong.

11

I am watching the wrong door. James could not believe his own foolishness. Eleanor had him turned inside out and upside down, that was the problem. Of course, no activity inside the house could be seen from here, in the square. No visitors would call this early. There was no call to open the front door.

The back would be a different matter. The main bedroom would look out over the garden. The cook and maids would be bustling around. There was possibly even a stable, where Eleanor had her carriage and horses. James would be able to scout the terrain, and discover whether the duchess was awake—perhaps even send up a note asking when he might call.

He leapt the fence into the street in a bound, and jogged along the row and down a narrow street beside the end townhouse. Xander let go of the leaves of a flowering cherry tree he had been idly mouthing and followed him.

As James came to the alley behind the houses, a carriage pulled away from a door further along the row. *I think that is Eleanor's house.* He'd have to count to be sure, and it could be some delivery and entirely innocent. Nonetheless, he broke into a run. Xander trotted to keep up.

It was the house, and the kitchen door had been left open. He called out, but had no reply. A quick sortie into the house confirmed no one was within. Not on the kitchen level, and not—when he climbed the stairs—in any of the public rooms or the bed chambers.

But in a large bedchamber at the rear of the house, he found a lady's clothing and other appurtenances, a bed with its covers tossed to the ground, and a chair, knocked over sideways.

Xander waited for him in the alley, dancing from hoof to hoof as he picked up his master's agitation.

James took a moment to hurry across to the mews. In the stable opposite the kitchen door, he found more evidence for his growing alarm. Two men, tied and gagged, occupied one of the stalls. He pulled his knife and released the hands of the one who was conscious. "Get free, look after your mate, and then go for the constables. Tell them the duchess has been kidnapped. I am going after her."

The man called after him as he left the stall. "Mrs Dorchester, Your Grace. Her Grace is calling herself Mrs Dorchester."

With a glint of humour he replied, "Then tell them Mr Dorchester has gone after her."

She would probably growl. His claim to be her husband would cause a scandal if her man could not be trusted. He would take a scolding with pleasure, for to berate him for his presumption, she would first need to be alive.

He was in Xander's saddle with the kind of bound the young men made to prove their strength and skill. Undoubtedly, his bones would complain later. For now, it had served his purpose—he was galloping at full speed down the narrow alley, grateful it was so early in the day, and any activity was taking place inside the stables on one side and the houses on the other.

When the alley let on to a broader road, he hesitated for a moment, then turned towards a boy who was slowly, and with little enthusiasm, sweeping the path. "Did you see a black carriage and pair a few minutes ago?" He pulled a coin from his pocket and tossed it in the air.

The boy watched its trajectory, and said, "Aye. Went right past me it did. The offside horse was white with brown patches. Very odd. Your horse is a strange one too. All shiny."

"Which way did it go from here?" James asked.

The boy pointed. "Turned into the road to Kenilworth, two corners along."

James tossed him the coin and set Xander back into a gallop.

The first two people he met on the Kenilworth road denied all knowledge of a dark cart pulled by a pair, one of which was white with brown patches. The girl in a goat cart loaded with bunches of flowers had noticed both carriage and horse, and pointed to a crossing ahead of him. "Passed me back on the corner, they did. At the rate you're going, Mister, you'll catch up soon enough."

But when he turned the corner into a long country lane, no vehicle was in sight.

He rode on, noting cart tracks and lesser paths as they branched off. The ground was too dry to show evidence of a recent passage, especially at his current speed. He kept going, wanting to be certain he was ahead of them before he turned back.

Ten minutes later, he pulled up. Xander should have overtaken a carriage and pair long before this. They had turned off. Provided the flower girl was telling the truth, but he'd have to trust her, for he had no other direction.

He returned more slowly, examining each way off the road as he reached it, occasionally riding a short distance down a path or a track before deciding his quarry had not used it.

He found an empty cottage and several with inhabitants, but none that had a building large enough to hide two horses and a carriage.

At last, quite close to the turn where he'd lost them, he found evidence that a vehicle had recently used a long and overgrown track. Not only was the grass pushed over and trampled down, but a fresh cluster of horse manure showed clear signs that a wheel had driven over it almost as soon as it was deposited.

When he looked along the track and saw a roof beyond a double row of trees, James dismounted and approached on foot. From the shelter of the trees, he saw a rundown farmhouse, with two horses grazing in a field alongside. One had a cream coat splotched in brown.

If the carriage was in the little barn, and James was prepared to bet that it was, he'd found his villains and his lady.

He left Xander loosely tethered among the trees, telling him to wait. If James called for the horse, he could easily break free, and if James was too long, the self-willed animal would come looking for him. Until either of those eventualities, only a lion or a pack of wolves would distract Xander from his duty to stay put. And this was gentle England, not the rugged mountains in which Xander had been raised.

James crept closer to the house, using every scrap of cover and listening for signs of life. Sure enough, the barn doors, hanging half off as they were, did not prevent him from seeing the carriage he had been chasing.

He worked his way around the house, looking cautiously into windows. Most of the rooms were empty. In the kitchen, two people were going at it like rabbits on the large farmhouse table. James ducked down, wrinkling his nose in distaste at the misuse of a food preparation area.

Then he stood to take a closer look. There was something familiar about the man. No. He couldn't quite place it. He knew the woman, though. Her face was distorted in her passion, but he had met her a dozen times recently. She was Eleanor's latest secretary, a Miss Grenford-Smith.

Some sort of flower name. Marigold! That was it. Eleanor trusted Marigold. Her current interactions with the presumed kidnapper suggested the trust was misplaced, and also explained how Eleanor had been kidnapped.

He continued his circuit of the house, and decided Eleanor must be on the upper level—a sloping roof that might contain a bedroom or two as well as storage space. He saw no one else. He should still be cautious in case of other confederates. Though would the couple in the kitchen be indulging as they were if others were in the house?

In his circuit, he had found a window with a broken catch. It was a moment's work and nearly silent to break it still further. Inside the room, he listened, but nothing disturbed the peace except the increasingly enthusiastic noises from the kitchen.

Carefully, checking each space before he moved to it, James made his way upstairs. Three doors. The first opened to an empty room, with nothing in it but dust and spiders. The second was certainly the major bedchamber of the house. James guessed that the kidnappers had co-opted it as their own, given the male and female clothing strewn around. So why they were not putting the bed to use, he could not imagine.

The third was locked, but he'd seen a key on a table beside the bed in the second room, so he fetched that and opened the door, his heart in his mouth, ready to attack a guard, fearing she was secured somewhere else.

Eleanor was there, alone, and unharmed. Relief froze him in the doorway, but he recovered quickly when she threw herself into his arms. He maneuvered her backwards, closing the door with one hand, while the other explored her to make sure she was real and unharmed.

The door shut, he crushed her to him and took her lips with his own, wild with relief. She was very real—a fragrant armful of human female, uncorseted and returning his kiss as enthusiastically as he could ever have imagined.

He was struggling to remember why he should pull away when she suddenly came to herself. "James, how did you find me? No! There's no time for that. Let's get away. Kit and Marigold are otherwise occupied, I imagine." Her voice dripped with scorn, as if James and Eleanor would never be so overcome by lust as to forget their role as guards.

Perhaps Eleanor wouldn't, but James couldn't be certain about himself. "They are otherwise occupied with great enthusiasm in the kitchen," he agreed. "From the sounds, they may be less occupied shortly."

Eleanor snorted. "So one would think, but I would not be surprised if they merely start again. They talked about it all the way from Leamington, and started in right outside my door. I had to bang quite loudly and for several minutes before Marigold complained I was putting her off and Kit took her downstairs. He is Elspeth Ashbury's boy, James. The one she took with her when she went into exile after betraying her brother. He thinks Haverford had her killed."

"So that's where I've seen him before! But let us go. You can tell me all about it when we are away from here." He looked at what she had on. A night rail and some sort of soft coat over it. "Let me steal something from the next room for you to wear."

She came with him, holding his hand. She chose a gown from the trunk that stood by the bed, and put it on over her night rail. "Her shoes won't fit me, James. Her feet are much smaller than mine."

"Never mind. I shall carry you if the ground is rough," he promised.

They crept down the stairs. The sounds from the kitchen suggested the couple had their second wind, and wouldn't hear the house falling down around their ears, but no point in taking any risks.

After that, it was simple. James retrieved Xander, and put Eleanor up before him. Out on the road, they met several mounted constables riding towards them, guided by Eleanor's groom. They directed them to the farmhouse, and gave the address of Eleanor's townhouse for the magistrate.

"We will leave you to it, gentlemen," James said. "I intend to take Mrs Dorchester home to rest after her ordeal."

"They will know who I am as soon as they arrest Kit and Marigold," Eleanor pointed out, as they rode away. "But they won't know who you are, James, so we can keep your name out of the scandal, if you wish."

"Do you want to know what I wish?" James asked, irritated by her suggestion that he could remain unaffected by anything that concerned her.

"Yes, of course."

"I want to take you back to the townhouse you have rented, lock all the doors, take you to bed, and show you those young people at the farmhouse had no expertise in what they were doing. And after that, I want to marry you, make you my duchess, and spend the rest of my life loving you."

Eleanor was silent. James leaned around her to see her face. "What do you think about that?" he asked.

"I have only one question," she answered.

He raised an eyebrow. "Which is?"

"How fast can this horse gallop with two of us on his back? I can hardly wait."

James nudged Xander into a run. Neither could he.

EPILOGUE

So Winshire and I are now married, dearest. Everyone outside of close family believes that the very quiet private ceremony took place before Leamington Prior, and not after. The Teatime Tattler *can make nothing of that, so has taken to calling me the Double Duchess.*

By the time you read this, the two miscreants will have been put on trial at the assizes. I felt rather sorry for them, but James says that, if they are sentenced to hang, it is only what they deserve. If Kit was angry about what happened to Elspeth, that did not justify his attempt to murder members of your family, which is quite true, dear, I agree. Even if you had given the order. Dear David made a point of telling Kit that the assassin was sent by that awful Stanley, her own brother.

As for Marigold, being made destitute by her selfish uncle was terrible, but I was only trying to help her. What a shame she had become so bitter and self-pitying that she was an easy prey for Kit when he realised that he could not reach any of your family without inside help.

In happier news, Jessica believes she is with child. Colyton and his daughters all hope it will be a son. Matilda's son has started to walk, and she thinks that another child might be on the way. How our family grows!

Speaking of which, I hope you and Cherry are well, and also Jonathan, his lovely wife, and all their babies. Do write soon to give me all your news.
With all my love
Eleanor Winshire.

THE END

AFTERWORD

You'll find the details of the story of how James and Eleanor became estranged, in *To Tame the Wild Rake*, the fourth novel in *The Return of the Mountain King*. See the next page for links.

One of my beta readers said that she'd have liked to see an intimate scene between James and Eleanor. I've written at least a little of this in a blog post for my regular blog feature, *Monday for Tea*, in which Eleanor has tea with another character from one of my books or, occasionally, from some other author's books.

See my post of 28 February for 'Tea with a lover'.

MORE IN THE MOUNTAIN KING SERIES

The Return of the Mountain King

James Winderfield, exiled third son of the Duke of Winshire, is back to inherit the ducal title

In 1812, high Society is rocked by the return of the Earl of Sutton, heir to the dying Duke of Winshire. James Winderfield, Earl of Sutton, Winshire's third and only surviving son, has long been thought dead, but his reappearance is not nearly such a shock as those he brings with him, the children of his deceased Persian-born wife and fierce armed retainers, both men and women.

The Duke of Haverford, his one-time rival in love, sets out to destroy him, and his children with him, but Sutton is no longer the friendless, open-hearted youth that was exiled for his temerity. Even inheriting his father's title won't stop his enemies from trying to kill him. But no one, his people whisper, ever wins against the King of the Mountains.

As the new Duke of Winshire's son, his daughter and his twin nieces navigate society to find acceptance and a love of their own, Winshire rekindles his acquaintance with the influential and beloved matriarch, Eleanor, Duchess of Haverford. Their time is long past; their friendship, though, is golden.

کمبل همه چیز برای عشق

To Wed a Proper Lady (Book 1) — The Barbarian and the Bluestocking

Everyone knows James needs a bride with impeccable blood lines. He needs Sophia's love more.

James, eldest son of the Earl of Sutton, must marry to please his grandfather, the Duke of Winshire, and to win social acceptance for himself and his father's other foreign-born children. But only Lady Sophia Belvoir makes his heart sing, and to win her, he must invite himself to spend Christmas at the home of his father's greatest enemy: the man who is fighting in Parliament to have his father's marriage declared invalid and the Winderfield children made bastards.

Sophia keeps secret her *tendre* for James, Lord Elfingham. After all, the whole of Society knows he is pursuing the younger Belvoir sister, not the older one left on the shelf after two failed betrothals. Even when he asks for her hand in marriage, she still can't quite believe that he loves her.

(This book was first published as a novella, and has been extensively rewritten to make it a novel. The novella was in the Bluestocking Belles' collection *Holly and Hopeful Hearts.*)

کمبل همه چیز برای عشق

A Suitable Husband

A chef from the slums, however talented, is no fit mate for the cousin of a duke, however distant. But Cedrica Grenford can dream. (novella)

کمبل همه چیز برای عشق

To Mend the Broken-Hearted (Book 2) — The Healer and the Hermit

Trained as a healer, Ruth Winderfield is happiest in a sickroom. When she's caught up in a smallpox epidemic and finds herself quarantined at the remote manor of a reclusive lord, the last thing she expects is to find her heart's desire. A pity he does not feel the same. She must return to London's ballrooms, where the wealth of her family and the question over her birth make her a target for the unscrupulous and a pariah to the high-sticklers.

Valentine, Earl of Ashbury, is horrified when an impertinent bossy female turns up with several sick children, including the two girls he is responsible for. He hasn't seen his niece and his daughter—if she is his daughter—since his faithless wife and treacherous brother died three years ago. He reluctantly gives them shelter. Even more reluctantly, he helps with the nursing.

When Ruth goes, she takes his heart with him. He must face his past and win her back, not just for himself, but for the children he has come to love.

کمبل همه چیز برای عشق

Melting Matilda (A novella in the Bluestocking Belle's collection, Fire & Frost, published as stand-alone in May 2021)

Sparks flew a year ago when the Granite Earl kissed the Ice Princess under the mistletoe. Matilda Grenford is a lady and the ward of a duchess, but the daughter of a famous courtesan. Charles, Earl of Hamner, seeks a countess of impeccable bloodlines, not one whose scandalous birth would offend every noble ancestor back to the Norman Conquest. But neither of them can forget that kiss.

کمبل همه چیز برای عشق

To Claim the Long-Lost Lover — The Diamond and the Doctor

Her girlhood lover is back, as compelling as ever, but Sarah Winderfield, Charlotte's twin, cannot forget he abandoned her, leaving her to face the anger of her family and worse. Sarah is even lovelier than when she was a girl, but Nate Beauclair has not forgiven her for betraying him to her father's revenge: press ganged to the navy and years of servitude.

To Tame the Wild Rake — The Saint and the Sinner

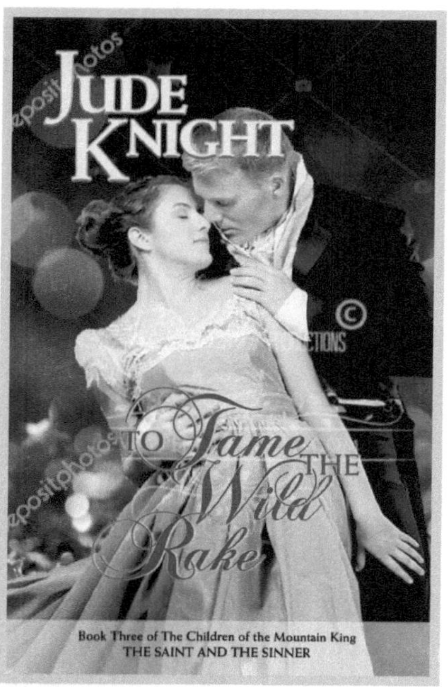

The Marquis of Aldridge doesn't want to yearn for the sister of a friend from his raking days. Especially since she has rejected him in no uncertain terms. Charlotte Winderfield, niece of the Mountain King, keeps a secret that bars her from marriage, but even if she found the courage to trust, she would never trust a rake.

کمبل همه چیز برای عشق

ABOUT THE AUTHOR

Jude has been trying to be a novelist since she was fourteen. She was a good enough reader to see that the first two attempts (one when she was fourteen and one in her early twenties) weren't good enough to publish. Then along came life. A seriously ill child who required years of therapy; a rising mortgage that led to a full-time job; her own chronic illness… the writing took a back seat.

As the years passed, the fear grew. She'd waited so long. If she never finished any of the dozens of novels she started, no one would ever judge them.

Jude's mother believed in her, and on the way home from that great lady's funeral, Jude realised she'd left it too late for her Mum to ever hold a print copy of one of her books. So she replaced the fear of finishing with the fear of not finishing, by telling everyone she knew that she was writing a novel.

In the five years from publishing her first fiction book in 2014, Jude published seven novels, thirteen novellas, a heap of shorter stories, and more novellas in group anthologies. She plans to keep going till she runs out of years.

Jude writes historical fiction with a large helping of romance, a splash of Regency, and a twist of suspense.

She then tries to figure out how to slot it into a genre category.

She's mad keen on history, enjoys what happens to people in the crucible of a passionate relationship, and loves to use a good mystery and some real danger as mechanisms to torture her characters.

In her other identity as Judy Knighton, she is a plain language consultant specialising in contracts, insurance policies, and financial disclosure statements. Fiction is more fun.

Website and blog: http://judeknightauthor.com/
Book blurbs and links: http://judeknightauthor.com/books/

کمبل همه چیز برای عشق

Do you like news before anyone else, plus discounts, and free stuff?

Sign up to Jude's newsletter. The main newsletter goes out once every two months, and includes news about coming books, discounts, contests, and events. Every newsletter also has news abut books from Jude's author friends, and a free story that Jude writes just for newsletter subscribers.

In between newsletters, if Jude has something exciting to share she occasionally sends a one-topic email.

Free book as a thank you

As a thank you for subscribing to Jude's newsletter, you can expect a series of three emails, the first offering a free copy of one of Jude's books, and the next two with links to other free stories. So why not subscribe today?

Subscribe to newsletter: http://judeknightauthor.com/newsletter/

کمبل همه چیز برای عشق

ALSO BY JUDE KNIGHT

lonely life. How hard can it be?

کمبل همه چیز برای عشق

Unkept Promises (Book 4 in *The Golden Redepennings* series)

Mia hopes to negotiate a comfortable marriage. Jules wants his wife to return to England, where she belongs. Love confounds them both.

کمبل همه چیز برای عشق

Other Regency books

A Baron for Becky

She was a fallen woman. How could the men who loved her help set her back on her feet?

کمبل همه چیز برای عشق

A Suitable Husband

A chef from the slums, however talented, is no fit mate for the cousin of a duke, however distant. But Cedrica can dream. (novella)

کمبل همه چیز برای عشق

House of Thorns

His rose thief bride comes with a scandal that threatens to tear them apart.

کمبل همه چیز برای عشق

Lord Calne's Christmas Ruby

One wealthy merchant's heiress with an aversion to fortune hunters. One an impoverished earl with a twisted hand. Combine and stir with one villainous rector. (novella)

کمبل همه چیز برای عشق

<u>*Revealed in Mist*</u>

As spy and enquiry agent, Prue and David worked to uncover secrets, while hiding a few of their own.

کمبل همه چیز برای عشق

<u>*The Beast Next Door*</u> (A novella in the Bluestocking Belles collection *Valentines from Bath)*

In all the assemblies and parties, no-one Charis met could ever match the beast next door.

کمبل همه چیز برای عشق

Lunch-length reads: story collections

<u>*Chasing the Tale*</u>

Escape into another place and time just long enough for a lunch or coffee break in eleven short stories from the imagination of award-winning author Jude Knight. Nine Regency plus one colonial New Zealand and one medieval Scotland. Multiple tropes, catastrophes and barriers on the way to a happy ending.

کمبل همه چیز برای عشق

<u>*Hand-Turned Tales*</u> and <u>*Lost in the Tale*</u>

A double handful of short stories and novellas, free from most eretailers. Try the range of Jude's imagination one bite at a time, in a lunch-length read.

کمبل همه چیز برای عشق

<u>*If Mistletoe Could Tell Tales*</u>

A repackaging of six published Christmas stories: four novellas and two novelettes. Because nothing enhances the magic of Christmas like the magic of love.

کمبل همه چیز برای عشق

Hearts in the Land of Ferns

Five stories all set in New Zealand: two historical and three contemporary suspense. All That Glisters has been published in Hand-Turned Tales. The other four have all been published in multi-author collections, but never before in a collection of Jude Knight stories.

کمبل همه چیز برای عشق

Victorian books

Never Kiss a Toad (with Mariana Gabrielle)

Caught together in her father's bed, Sally and Toad are wrenched apart, to endure years of separation. But neither distance nor malice can destroy true love.

کمبل همه چیز برای عشق

God Help Ye, Merry Gentleman (with Mariana Gabrielle)

A Christmas collection: two purpose-written short pieces in the world of *Never Kiss a Toad*, showing Sally's and Toad's childhood and youth. Plus some other published pieces from blogs, newsletters, and books set in the same world.

کمبل همه چیز برای عشق

Forged in Fire (novella in the Bluestocking Belles collection *Never Too Late)*

Burned in their youth, neither Tad nor Lottie expected to feel the fires of love. Until the inferno of a volcanic eruption sears away the lies of the past and frees them to forge a new future.

کمبل همه چیز برای عشق

Post-apocalyptic fiction

A Midwinter's Tale (novella in the Speakeasy Scribes collection *Resist and Rejoice)*

Verity Marchand is an orphan of time, her family tavern under the ice that grips Boston. When Verity's dreams lead her into a nightmare, she'll need a miracle—or the family cat—to save her.

کمبل همه چیز برای عشق

Contemporary

*A Family Christmas (*novella in the Authors of Main Street collection *Christmas Babies on Main Street)*

Kirilee is on the run, in disguise, out of touch, and eating for two. Trevor is heading home for Christmas, after three years undercover, investigating a global criminal organisation. In the heart of a storm, two people from different worlds question what divides and what unites them.

کمبل همه چیز برای عشق

Abbie's Wish (novella in the Authors of Main Street collection *Christmas Wishes on Main Street)*

Abbie's Christmas wish draws three men to her mother. One of them is a monster.

کمبل همه چیز برای عشق

Beached (novella in the Authors of Main Street collection *Summer Romance on Main Street)*

The truth will wash away her coastal paradise

کمبل همه چیز برای عشق

The Gingerbread Caper (novella in the Authors of Main Street collection *Christmas Cookies on Main Street)*

A mischievous cat, a spy mystery, a gingerbread-munching burglar, a Christmas challenge gone wrong, and a tender new love. All in a New Zealand seaside resort.